LOUISA MAY ALCOTT'S

LITTLE WOMEN

ALSO BY LAURA WOOD

Jane Austen's Pride & Prejudice: A Retelling

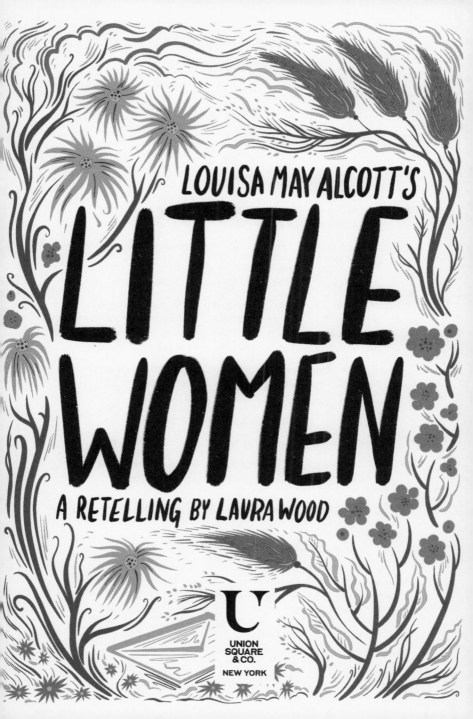

LOUISA MAY ALCOTT'S

LITTLE WOMEN

A RETELLING BY LAURA WOOD

U

UNION SQUARE & CO.

NEW YORK

**UNION
SQUARE
& CO.**

NEW YORK

UNION SQUARE & CO. and the distinctive Union Square & Co. logo are trademarks of Sterling Publishing Co., Inc.

Union Square & Co., LLC, is a subsidiary of Sterling Publishing Co., Inc.

Text © 2023 Laura Wood
Cover illustration © 2025 Helen Crawford-White

First published in Great Britain in 2023 by Barrington Stoke Ltd.
First published in the United States and Canada in 2025
by Union Square & Co., LLC.

ISBN 978-1-4549-5853-6

Library of Congress Control Number: 2024938253

For information about custom editions, special sales, and premium purchases, please contact specialsales@unionsquareandco.com.

Printed in China

2 4 6 8 10 9 7 5 3 1

unionsquareandco.com

Union Square & Co.'s EVERYONE CAN BE A READER books are expertly written, thoughtfully designed with dyslexia-friendly fonts and paper tones, and carefully formatted to meet readers where they are with engaging stories that encourage reading success across a wide range of age and interest levels.

Little Women was the first book I ever took out of the library and it lit a fire in me that's been burning ever since, so I'd like to dedicate this book to the librarians who probably don't know just how many lives they're changing.

1.

"Christmas won't be Christmas without any presents," Jo grumbled, lying on the rug.

"It's so dreadful to be poor!" Meg sighed, looking down at her old dress.

"I don't think it's fair for some girls to have lots of pretty things and other girls to have nothing at all," little Amy added, sticking out her bottom lip.

"We've got Father and Mother, and each other," Beth said from her corner.

They all smiled at Beth's words, but then those smiles turned to frowns. They had remembered their father was away where the war was being fought.

The firelight shone on the March sisters and their four very different faces. There was Meg, the oldest, who was sixteen. Meg was pretty with dark hair and wide gray eyes, and she thought herself very grown up and in charge.

Meg spent a lot of time being worried. Sometimes she was worried about her sisters; sometimes she was worried about her parents. Other times she couldn't help being worried about all the nice things that sixteen-year-old girls were supposed to have that she didn't—things like pretty dresses and silk stockings and satin gloves.

After Meg there was Jo, who was fifteen. Jo was tall and skinny and let everyone see her emotions. If Jo was cross, then her scowl was fierce and it felt like a thunderstorm rolling in. If she was happy, then her smile seemed to brighten up the whole room. Jo had long, beautiful chestnut hair that her sisters were jealous of but that Jo didn't seem to care about one bit.

The next sister was Beth. Beth was thirteen and she had soft brown hair and soft brown eyes. Every bit of Beth was soft, because Beth was the sweetest girl in the whole world, as Jo was fond of saying.

Finally, there was Amy, who was twelve. Amy looked like a china doll with clear blue eyes and blond curls. It was clear that one day she would be very beautiful. As the youngest, Amy was a little spoiled. She was very worried about making sure she wasn't left out of any adventures her sisters might take on.

Nobody spoke for a minute as they thought about Father being away. Then Meg said, "You know the reason Mother said we shouldn't have any presents this Christmas was because it's going to be a hard winter for everyone. She thinks we shouldn't spend money on ourselves when people are suffering. We can't do much, but we can make our little sacrifices and should do it gladly." Meg shook her head and added, "Well, that's what they say, but I'm afraid I don't make my sacrifices gladly. I'm not glad about them at all."

"But I do think we should be able to spend our own pocket money," said Jo. "I really do want a new book."

"I planned to spend mine on new music," said Beth with a little sigh that no one heard.

"I shall get a nice box of drawing pencils. I really need them," said Amy.

"Mother didn't say anything about our pocket money," cried Jo. "She won't wish us to give up *everything*. Let's each buy what we want and have a little fun. I'm sure we work hard enough to earn it."

"I know I do, teaching those tiresome children nearly all day," said Meg, who tutored Mr. and Mrs. King's young daughters.

"You don't have half such a hard time as I do," said Jo. "How would you like to spend hours with a nervous, fussy old lady who keeps you running around and is never satisfied?" Jo's job was looking after Aunt March, who really was very grumpy.

"I know I shouldn't complain," Beth said, "but I do think washing dishes and keeping things tidy is the worst work in the world. It makes me cross, and my hands get so stiff I can't practice the piano well at all."

"I don't believe any of you suffer as I do," cried Amy dramatically. "You don't have to go to school with awful girls who make fun of you if you don't know your lessons and laugh at your dresses. They say mean things about your father if he isn't rich, and insult you when your nose isn't nice."

Here, Amy pinched her nose. It was perfectly nice, but Amy thought it was not small or turned-up enough. Sometimes Amy held her nose in a clothes pin to try to change it, but so far the results of this experiment had been unpromising.

"Don't you wish we had the money Father lost when we were little, Jo?" said Meg. "Dear me! How happy and good we'd be if we had no worries!"

"You said the other day you thought *we* were a lot happier than the King children," Beth piped up, "because they were always fighting, in spite of their money."

"Well, I think we are happier," Meg admitted. "We might have to work, but we make fun of ourselves and are a pretty jolly set, as Jo would say."

"Jo does use such slang words!" Amy said, giving a disapproving look to Jo stretched out on the rug.

Jo sat up, put her hands in her pockets, and began to whistle.

"Don't, Jo. Whistling is so boyish!" Amy scolded.

"That's why I do it." Jo stuck out her tongue.

"I detest rude, unladylike girls!" Amy exclaimed.

"I hate stuck-up little children!" Jo snapped.

"Sisters are the best of friends," sang Beth, the peacemaker. She made such a funny face that Jo's and Amy's sharp voices softened to a laugh and the argument ended.

"Really, girls, you are both to be blamed," said Meg. As the oldest, she felt it was her job to keep the others in line. "Amy, you must stop being such a know-it-all, and, Jo, you are too old to be playing boyish tricks. It didn't matter so much when you were a little girl, but now you are so tall and tie up your hair you should remember that you are a young lady."

"I'm not!" cried Jo. "And if wearing my hair up makes me one, then I'll wear it in pigtails until I'm twenty." She pulled the pins from her hair and shook out her long waves. "I hate to think I've got to grow up. It's bad enough to be a girl, anyway. And it's worse than ever now, because I'm dying to go and fight with Father. And I can only stay home and knit, like a poky old woman!"

And Jo shook the lumpy-looking blue sock she was knitting until the needles rattled and her ball of wool bounded across the room.

They were interrupted by the clock striking six. Beth put a pair of slippers down to warm by the fire. Somehow this had a good effect upon the girls because it meant the return of Marmee, which was what they all called their mother.

Meg stopped lecturing and lit the lamp, Amy got out of the easy chair without being asked, and Jo forgot how tired she was, holding up the slippers nearer to the blaze.

"These slippers are quite worn out. Marmee must have a new pair," Jo said.

"I thought I'd get her some with my dollar," said Beth.

"No, I shall!" cried Amy.

"I'm the oldest," began Meg.

But Jo cut in with "I'm the man of the family now Father is away. I shall provide the slippers, for he told me to take special care of Marmee while he was gone."

"I'll tell you what we could do," said Beth. "Let's each get Marmee something for Christmas and not get anything for ourselves."

"What will we get?" exclaimed Jo.

Everyone thought for a minute. Then Meg announced, "I shall give her a nice pair of gloves."

"New slippers, the best to be had," cried Jo.

"Some handkerchiefs, all hemmed," said Beth.

"I'll get a little bottle of perfume," added Amy. "Marmee likes it, and it won't cost much, so I'll have some left to buy my pencils."

"Glad to find you so merry, my girls," said a cheery voice at the door. The sisters all stopped talking at once, careful to make sure their plans weren't overheard.

"Well, dearies, how have you got on today?" Marmee asked. "There was so much to do that I didn't come home to dinner. Has anyone called, Beth? How is your cold, Meg? Jo, you look tired to death. Come and kiss me, Amy." Marmee bustled in, her cheeks pink, and she was wrapped up in a shabby gray coat.

The girls flew about, trying to make things comfortable. Meg arranged the tea table, and Jo brought wood and set chairs, dropping and clattering everything she touched. Beth trotted out to the kitchen and back, quiet and busy. Meanwhile Amy gave directions to everyone as she sat with her hands folded.

They gathered about the table for tea, and Mrs. March said, with a happy face, "I've got a treat for you after supper."

Smiles flashed on their faces like a streak of sunshine. Beth clapped her hands, and Jo tossed up her napkin, crying, "A letter! A letter! Three cheers for Father!"

"Yes, a nice long letter," said Marmee. "He is well and thinks he shall get past the cold season better than we feared. Father sends all sorts of loving wishes for Christmas and a special message to you girls." Marmee patted her pocket as if she had a treasure there.

"Hurry and get done eating!" cried Jo. "Don't stop to quirk your little finger and simper over your plate, Amy." She choked on her tea and dropped her bread, butter side down, on the carpet.

"I wish I could have gone to the war as a drummer, or a nurse," Jo continued. "Then I could be near Father and help him."

"It must be very disagreeable to sleep in a tent, and eat all sorts of bad-tasting things, and drink out of a tin mug," sighed Amy.

"When will Father come home, Marmee?" asked Beth with a quiver in her voice.

"Not for many months, dear, unless he is sick. Your father will stay and do his work as long as he can, and we won't ask for him back a minute sooner than he can be spared. Now come and hear the letter."

They all drew to the fire. Marmee was in the big chair with Beth at her feet. Meg and Amy were perched on either arm of the chair, and Jo leaned on the back, where no one would see any sign of emotion if the letter should be touching.

It was a cheerful, hopeful letter, full of lively descriptions of camp life, marches, and military news. Only at the end did it become sentimental:

Give the girls all of my love and a kiss. Tell them I think of them all the time. A year seems very long to wait before I see them, but remind them that while we wait we may all work so that these hard days need not be wasted. I know they will remember all I said to them, that when I come back to them I may be fonder and prouder than ever of my little women.

They were all emotional after that. Even Jo wasn't ashamed of the great tear that dropped off the end of her nose.

2.

Jo was the first to wake in the gray dawn of Christmas morning. She stretched out in bed and listened to the soft silence of the snowy day for a moment. It was strange to think about Christmas without Father there, much stranger even than Christmas without presents.

"Where is Marmee?" asked Meg as she and Jo ran downstairs.

"Goodness only knows," replied Hannah. She had lived with the family since Meg was born and was considered by them all more as a friend than a servant. "Some poor little lad came asking for help, and your ma went straight off to see what was needed. There never was such a woman for giving things away even when she's nothing to spare herself."

"She'll be back soon, I think. Let's have everything ready," said Meg. She looked over the presents kept under the sofa in a basket, ready to be produced at the perfect moment. "Where is Amy's bottle of perfume?" Meg asked.

"She took it out a minute ago and went off to put a ribbon on it, or something," replied Jo.

"How nice my handkerchiefs look, don't they?" said Beth. "Hannah washed and ironed them for me."

"There's Marmee. Hide the basket, quick!" cried Jo as a door slammed and steps sounded in the hall.

But instead of Marmee, Amy came rushing in.

"Where have you been and what are you hiding behind you?" Meg asked Amy. She was surprised to see that lazy Amy had been out so early, going by her hood and cloak.

"I changed the small bottle of perfume for the big one, and I gave all my money to get it," Amy said breathlessly. "I'm truly trying not to be selfish any more." She had spent a long, hard night thinking about Father's letter and feeling strangely worried that he wouldn't be very proud of her at the moment.

As she spoke, Amy showed the handsome perfume bottle that replaced the cheap one. She looked so earnest and humble in her little effort to forget herself that Meg hugged her on the spot and

Jo pronounced her "a real hero." Meanwhile Beth ran to the window and picked her finest rose to place with the stately bottle.

They had just hidden the basket of presents away again as the front door swung open and Marmee came bustling in.

"Merry Christmas, little daughters!" Marmee said. "I want to say one word before we sit down to eat. Not far away from here lies a family called the Hummels. There is a poor woman with a little newborn baby. Six children are huddled into one bed to keep from freezing, because they have no fire. There's nothing to eat over there, and the oldest boy came to tell me they were suffering hunger and cold. My girls, will you give them your breakfast as a Christmas present?"

For a moment there was a stunned silence. The Christmas breakfast was laid out waiting for them like a treat, and they had been looking forward to it for a long time. They were all very hungry, having waited nearly an hour for Marmee to get back. For a minute no one spoke.

Then Jo cleared her throat and exclaimed, "I'm so glad you came before we began!"

"May I go and help carry the things to the poor little children?" asked Beth eagerly.

"I shall take the cream and the muffins," added Amy, giving up the treats she most liked.

Meg was already covering the cakes and piling the bread onto one big plate.

"I thought you'd do it," said Mrs. March, smiling as if satisfied. "You will all come and help me, and when we come back we can have bread and milk for breakfast. We'll make it up at dinnertime, I promise. I'm so proud of my kind girls."

They were soon ready, and the procession set out. When they reached the house, the girls stopped speaking. It was a poor, bare, miserable room, with broken windows, no fire, and ragged bedclothes. They saw the sick mother, a wailing baby, and a group of pale, hungry children huddled under one old quilt, trying to keep warm.

"Oh! It is good angels come to help us!" said the poor woman.

"Funny angels in hoods and mittens," said Jo. She pulled a silly face and that made the little children giggle, which made things seem suddenly a lot less terrible.

In a few minutes their kindness transformed the room. Hannah made a fire with the wood she'd carried and stopped up the broken windows with old hats and her own cloak. Mrs. March gave the mother tea and porridge, and comforted her with promises of help. Then she dressed the little baby as tenderly as if it had been her own. The girls spread the table, gathered the children around the fire, and fed them like they were hungry birds, laughing and talking.

That was a very happy breakfast, though the girls didn't get any of it themselves. And when they left, they were the merriest four people in all the city.

Back at home, the girls were determined to give Marmee her gifts. While she ran upstairs to change, the March sisters arranged the gifts carefully on the table, a beautiful vase of red roses placed carefully in the middle.

"She's coming!" cried Jo, prancing about. "Strike up the music, Beth! Open the door, Amy! Three cheers for Marmee!"

Beth played a cheerful tune on the old wheezy piano, Amy threw open the door, and Meg bowed before showing Marmee in like she was the guest of honor.

Marmee was very surprised, and her smile was huge. Her eyes shone brightly as she examined her presents and read the little notes that accompanied them. The slippers went on at once, a new handkerchief scented with Amy's perfume was slipped into her pocket, and the nice gloves were pronounced a perfect fit.

There was a good deal of laughing and kissing, but the girls didn't have long to relax because there was a very important tradition to prepare for: the March Sisters' Christmas Production.

3.

Every year the four girls put on a spectacular play on Christmas Day and invited their friends from school to come and watch. Each year Jo's ambitions got greater and greater, so there was much excitement in the chattering group of young ladies who arrived that afternoon.

A dozen girls piled onto the bed and sat waiting before the blue-and-yellow curtains. There was a good deal of rustling and whispering behind the curtains, a bit of lamp smoke, and the odd giggle from Amy, who did tend to get hysterical in the excitement of the moment.

The March sisters had been doing this for years. Jo often complained that she didn't have the budget to bring her true vision to life, but the girls made whatever they needed. Some of their props were very clever: pasteboard guitars, antique lamps made of butter boats covered with silver paper, and gorgeous robes of old cotton glittering with tin lids from a pickle factory.

No gentleman was admitted, either in the audience or on stage, and so Jo played the boys' parts to her heart's content. She took immense satisfaction in wearing a pair of leather boots given to her by a friend who knew a lady who knew an actor. These boots, an old sword, and a slashed doublet were Jo's chief treasures. They appeared in every play the sisters did.

The fact that there were only four actors made it necessary for Jo and Meg to take several parts each. They whisked in and out of various costumes as well as managing the stage.

Soon, a bell sounded, the curtains flew apart, and the performance began.

A sign appeared, held from the edge of the stage in a wobbling hand. It said: "A gloomy wood" in large letters, and then was pulled away, revealing the scene.

There were a few plants in pots, green cloth on the floor, and a cave in the distance. This cave was made with a clothes rack for a roof and chests of drawers for walls. In the cave was a small furnace at full blast, with a black pot on it that an old witch was bending over. The stage was dark, and the glow of the furnace had a fine effect, especially as real steam came from the kettle when the witch took off the cover.

A moment was allowed for the first thrill from the audience to subside, then Hugo, the villain, stalked in. He had a clanking sword at his side, a slouching hat, black beard, mysterious cloak, and the boots. This was Jo, of course, and her eyes sparkled with pleasure.

Jo paced to and fro, clearly agitated, then struck her forehead. She burst out in a very loud and very enthusiastic song, singing of her hatred for the character Roderigo, her love for the character Zara, and her pleasing decision to kill one and win the other.

The high drama of the scene was very impressive, and the audience applauded as soon as Jo paused for breath. She bowed as if she received this public praise often, then moved to the cavern. There, Jo ordered the witch to come forth with a commanding "What ho, minion! I need thee!"

Meg hobbled over, dressed as the witch. She had gray horsehair hanging about her face, a red-and-black robe, and a staff in her hand. Jo demanded a potion from the witch to make Zara adore her, and one to destroy Roderigo.

In a very fine voice, Meg sang a song to call out Amy, who was dressed as a sparkly little cherub complete with wings. She strutted across the stage, smiling brilliantly at the audience, and handed Meg a small bottle. She then began an impromptu dance routine.

"That's enough!" Jo hissed out the corner of her mouth. Amy threw a handful of gold foil in the air, some of which got caught in Jo's beard, much to her disgust. Only then did Amy finally spin away.

Beth crept onto the stage like a shadow not really wishing to be seen, dressed as an imp with her face painted green. Shyly, Beth handed Meg another bottle and then slipped away without a word. Meg gave the bottles to Jo, who sang something long and complicated about her gratitude, then put the potions in her boots.

Jo departed, and Meg informed the audience in a very witchy voice that she had cursed Jo's character, as he had killed a few of her friends in times past. She intended to thwart his plans and be revenged on him. There were loud gasps and cheers, and then the curtain fell for the interval, and the audience lay back on the bed and ate sweets while discussing the merits of the play.

A good deal of hammering went on before the curtain rose again.

The carpentry it revealed was truly superb. A tower rose to the ceiling, halfway up appeared a window with a lamp burning in it, and behind the white curtain appeared Amy. She was playing the part of Zara in a lovely blue-and-silver dress, waiting for Roderigo.

He made a gorgeous entrance, with a plumed cap, a red cloak, chestnut hair, a guitar, and the boots, of course. It seemed Jo was playing both the hero and the villain in the play, and she was enjoying herself very much.

Kneeling at the foot of the tower, Jo sang a serenade in melting tones. Amy replied and, after more singing, agreed to fly down.

Then came the grand effect of the play. Jo produced a rope ladder with five steps to it, threw up one end and invited Amy to descend. Timidly she crept from her window and put her hand on Roderigo's shoulder. She was about to leap gracefully down when she forgot her long dress. The dress caught in the window, the tower tottered, leaned forward, fell with a crash and buried the unhappy lovers in the ruins.

A shriek rose from the audience as the boots waved wildly from the wreck. A golden head appeared exclaiming, "I told you so! I told you so!"

Meg, dressed as Don Pedro, the cruel father, rushed in. Thinking quickly, she dragged out Amy, while hissing, "Don't laugh! Act as if it was all right!" Then she made up a whole song on the spot in which she told Jo off for trying to steal Amy away.

Jo was certainly shaken by the fall of the tower upon her. Yet she rose magnificently to the occasion and strode around the stage shouting that she would never surrender, waving her sword around for effect.

Meg called for a servant to come and take the pair away. Beth came in with chains and led them away, looking very much frightened and clearly forgetting the speech she should have made. The more observant members of the audience would have noticed the stubborn streaks of green around her hair, but no one was rude enough to mention it.

After this, the rest of the play went off without a hitch. Indeed several of the audience were reduced to tears by Jo's very touching performance as Roderigo when he thought Zara had abandoned him. All cheered when Jo spent a good five minutes drawing out the evil Hugo's death scene.

At the end of the performance, the cast came out to take their bows. The audience clapped so wildly that the folding bed they sat on collapsed and folded inward, swallowing them all up.

With much laughter, the cast rescued the audience, and everyone proclaimed it the best play they had ever seen. The excitement still remained when Hannah appeared to give "Mrs. March's compliments, and would the ladies walk down to supper."

This was a surprise even to the actors. When they saw the table, they looked at one another with amazement. It was like Marmee to offer a little treat for them, but anything so fine as this was unheard of.

There was ice cream—actually two dishes of it, pink and white—and cake and fruit and distracting French bonbons. In the middle of the table were four great bouquets of greenhouse flowers.

It took their breath away, and they stared first at the table and then at their mother. Marmee looked as if she enjoyed their surprise immensely.

"Is it fairies?" asked Amy.

"Santa Claus," said Beth.

"Marmee did it," said Meg, and gave her sweetest smile, in spite of her gray beard and white eyebrows.

"Aunt March had a good fit and sent the supper," Jo guessed.

"All wrong. Our neighbor Mr. Laurence sent it," replied Marmee.

"What in the world put such a thing into his head? We don't know him!" exclaimed Meg.

"Hannah told one of his servants about your breakfast party," Marmee explained. "Mr. Laurence is an odd old gentleman, but that pleased him. He knew my father years ago, and he sent me a polite note this afternoon, saying he hoped I would allow him to express his friendly feeling toward my children by sending them a few trifles in honor of the day. I could not refuse, and so now you have a little feast to make up for the bread-and-milk breakfast." Marmee smiled.

"His grandson put it into his head, I know he did!" Jo exclaimed. "He is staying with Mr. Laurence. He looks as if he'd like to know us, but he's shy. Besides, Meg is so prim she won't let me speak to him when we pass."

As Jo spoke, the plates went round and the ice cream began to melt out of sight, with oohs and aahs of satisfaction.

"You mean the people who live in the big house next door, don't you?" asked one of the guests. "My mother knows old Mr. Laurence but says he's very proud and doesn't like to mix with his neighbors. He keeps his grandson shut up, when he isn't riding or walking with his tutor, and makes him study very hard. We invited him to our party, but he didn't come. Mother says his grandson is very nice, but he never speaks to us girls."

"Our cat ran away once, and he brought her back," said Jo. "We talked over the fence, and were getting on very well, chatting all about cricket. But then he saw Meg coming and walked off. He needs fun, I'm sure he does."

"I like his manners, and he looks like a little gentleman," Marmee said. "I've no objection to your knowing him, if a proper opportunity comes. He brought the flowers himself, and I should have asked him in if I had been sure what was going on upstairs. He looked so wistful as he went away, hearing your fun and having none of his own."

"It's a good job you didn't invite him in!" laughed Jo, looking at her boots. "But we'll perform another play sometime that he can see. Perhaps he'll help act. Wouldn't that be jolly?"

"I never had such a fine bouquet before! How pretty it is!" Meg said, examining her flowers with great interest.

"They are lovely. But the roses from Beth are sweeter to me," said Mrs. March, smelling the half-dead flowers in her belt.

Beth nestled up to her and whispered softly, "I wish I could send my bunch to Father. I don't think he's having such a merry Christmas as we are."

4.

"Jo! Jo! Where are you?" cried Meg at the foot of the stairs.

"Here!" answered a husky voice from above. Running up, Meg found her sister eating apples and crying over her book, wrapped up in a blanket on an old three-legged sofa by the window.

This was Jo's favourite place. She loved to sit here with half a dozen apples and a nice book, to enjoy the quiet and the company of a pet rat who lived nearby and didn't mind her a bit. As Meg appeared, Scrabble the rat whisked into his hole. Jo shook the tears off her cheeks and waited to hear the news from Meg.

"An invitation from Mrs. Gardiner for tomorrow night!" cried Meg, waving the precious paper and then reading it with girlish delight.

"'Mrs. Gardiner would be happy to see Miss Meg and Miss Josephine at a little dance on New Year's

Eve,'" Meg said breathlessly. "Marmee says we may go, now what shall we wear?"

"What's the point of asking that when you know we shall wear our only good dresses?" answered Jo with her mouth full. "We haven't got anything else!"

"If I only had a silk gown!" sighed Meg. "Marmee says I may when I'm eighteen perhaps, but two years is an everlasting time to wait."

"I'm sure our dresses *look* like silk, and they're nice enough for us. Yours is as good as new." Jo stopped talking then and frowned as if remembering something. "But I forgot mine has a burn and a tear. What shall I do? The burn shows badly in the back."

"You'll just have to sit still all you can and keep your back out of sight," Meg said. "The front is all right. I shall have a new ribbon for my hair, and Marmee will lend me her little pearl pin. My new slippers are lovely, and my gloves will do, even if they aren't as nice as I'd like." Meg spoke dreamily, already imagining the lovely picture she would make.

"I spilled lemonade on my gloves, and I can't get any new ones, so I shall have to go without," said Jo, who never troubled herself much about what she wore.

"You must have gloves or I won't go," cried Meg. "Gloves are more important than anything else. You can't dance without them, and if you don't dance, I should be so mortified."

"Then I'll stay still," Jo said. "I don't care much for dancing at parties. It's no fun to go calmly sailing round. I like to fly about. No! I'll tell you how we can manage—each wear one good one and carry a bad one. Don't you see?" Jo grinned, pleased to have solved the problem.

"Your hands are bigger than mine, and you will stretch my glove dreadfully," began Meg, whose gloves were a tender point with her.

"Then I'll go without. I don't care what people say!" Jo shrugged, picking up her book.

"You may have one of my gloves, you may!" said Meg. "Only don't stain it and do behave nicely. Don't put your hands behind you or stare, will you?" Meg's voice was anxious.

"Don't worry about me," Jo said. "I'll be as prim as I can and not get into any scrapes, if I can help it. Now go and answer your invitation and let me finish this splendid story."

So Meg went away to "accept with thanks" and look over her dress. Meanwhile Jo finished her story and her four apples, and had a game of romps with Scrabble.

When New Year's Eve came, the parlor was deserted. Amy and Beth were too young to be invited to the dance, but they played at dressing maids to help their older sisters with the important business of "getting ready for the party." The outfits were simple, yet there was a great deal of running up and down, laughing and talking, and at one time a strong smell of burnt hair filled the house.

Meg wanted a few pretty curls about her face. Jo took charge, rolling the hair up into bits of paper and then pinching them with a pair of hot tongs warmed in the fire.

"Should they be smoking like that?" asked Beth from her perch on the bed.

"It's the dampness drying," replied Jo with great confidence.

"What a funny smell!" observed Amy, smoothing her own pretty curls.

"There, now I'll take off the papers and you'll see a cloud of little ringlets," said Jo, putting down the tongs with satisfaction.

She did take off the papers, but no cloud of ringlets appeared, because the hair came away with the papers. The horrified hairdresser laid a row of little scorched bundles on the table before her victim.

"Oh, oh, oh! What have you done? I'm spoiled! I can't go! My hair, oh, my hair!" wailed Meg. She looked with despair at the uneven frizzle on her forehead.

"Just my luck!" groaned poor Jo. "You shouldn't have asked me to do it. I always spoil everything. I'm so sorry, but the tongs were too hot, and so I've made a mess."

"It isn't spoiled," said Amy. "Just frizzle it and tie your ribbon so the ends come on your forehead a bit, and it will look like the last fashion. I've seen many girls do it so."

"Serves me right for trying to be fine. I wish I'd let my hair alone," cried Meg.

"It will soon grow out again," said Beth, coming to kiss and comfort the shorn sheep.

After various smaller mishaps, Meg was finished at last, and Jo's hair was pulled up and her dress on.

They looked lovely, Meg in a silver dress with her hair pinned up and arranged to hide the missing curls, and Jo in maroon with a stiff, gentlemanly linen collar. Each put on one nice light glove and carried one dirty one.

Meg's high-heeled slippers were very tight and pinched her feet dreadfully, but she would never, ever say so. Jo's nineteen hairpins all seemed stuck straight into her head, which was not exactly comfortable. But Jo only grinned and said, "Dear me, let us be elegant or die."

"Have a good time, dearies!" called Marmee as the sisters left the house. "Have you both got nice pocket handkerchiefs?"

"Yes, yes!" cried Jo. She added with a laugh as they left, "I do believe Marmee would ask about our handkerchiefs if we were all running away from an earthquake."

"It is one of her aristocratic tastes, and quite proper," replied Meg. "A real lady is always known by neat boots, gloves, and handkerchief." She had a good many little "aristocratic tastes" of her own.

They reached Mrs. Gardiner's house quickly, but before they went inside Jo tugged on Meg's arm.

"If you see me doing anything wrong, just remind me with a wink, will you?" said Jo, giving her collar a twitch and her head a hasty brush.

"No, winking isn't ladylike," Meg said. "I'll lift my eyebrows if anything is wrong and nod if you are all right. Now hold your shoulders straight, and take short steps, and *don't* shake hands if you are introduced to anyone. It isn't the thing."

"How do you learn all the proper ways?" Jo grumbled as they entered the party. "I never can. Isn't that music nice?"

In they went, feeling a bit shy because they rarely went to parties. This little gathering might have been informal, but it was a big event to them.

Mrs. Gardiner was a stately old lady who greeted them kindly. Meg was quickly swallowed up by a group of young ladies.

Jo didn't care much for girls or girlish gossip and stood about with her back carefully against the wall, feeling very out of place. Some cheerful lads were talking about skates in another part of the room, and she longed to go and join them, because skating was one of the joys of her life.

Jo caught Meg's eye and nodded toward the boys, but Meg's eyebrows went up so alarmingly that Jo dared not move. No one came to talk to her, and she could not wander about and amuse herself because her burnt dress would show, so she stared at people rather sadly until the dancing began.

Meg was asked to dance at once. Her tight slippers tripped about so fast that nobody would have guessed the pain she was feeling.

Jo saw a big red-headed boy approaching her corner. Fearing he meant to ask her to dance, she slipped behind a pair of heavy curtains, hoping just to be able to peep out and enjoy watching the party in peace.

Behind the curtains was a small space with two straight-backed chairs inside it. In one of those chairs was a boy. The boy was the same age as Jo and tall, with curly black hair, big dark eyes, and a very handsome nose. It was Mr. Laurence's grandson, the boy who lived next door to them, and he looked as surprised as Jo.

"Dear me, I didn't know anyone was here!" stammered Jo. She was about to move back out as fast as she had bounced in.

But the boy laughed and said pleasantly, "Don't mind me. Stay if you like. I only came here because I don't know many people and felt a bit awkward, you know."

"So did I," Jo replied, smiling. "I think I've had the pleasure of seeing you before. You live near us, don't you?"

"Next door," he said, and he looked up and laughed. He found Jo's prim manner rather funny when he remembered how they had chatted about cricket when he'd brought the cat home.

Jo relaxed and she laughed too as she said, "We did have such a good time over your nice Christmas present."

"Grandpa sent it," the boy said.

"But you put it into his head, didn't you now?" Jo replied.

"How is your cat, Miss March?" asked the boy. He was trying to look serious while his black eyes shone with fun.

"Very well, thank you, Mr. Laurence. But I am not Miss March, I'm only Jo."

"I'm not Mr. Laurence, I'm only Laurie," Laurie said.

"Laurie Laurence, what an odd name." Jo wrinkled her nose.

"My first name is Theodore," Laurie told her. "But I don't like it, so I make people call me Laurie instead."

"I hate my name too—it's so sentimental! I wish everyone would say Jo instead of Josephine." Jo sighed.

Laurie grinned. "You are definitely a Jo not a Josephine."

"That is the nicest thing you could possibly say," Jo replied.

"Don't you like to dance, Jo?" asked Laurie.

"I like it if there is plenty of room and everyone is lively. In a place like this I'm sure to knock something over, tread on people's toes, or do something dreadful. So I keep out of mischief and let Meg sail about. Don't you dance?"

"If you will come too," Laurie answered with a little bow.

"I can't, because I told Meg I wouldn't, because . . ." Jo stopped. She didn't know whether to tell him the truth or to start laughing.

"Because what?" Laurie asked, intrigued.

"You won't tell?" Jo lifted her eyebrows.

"Never!" Laurie swore.

"Well, I have a bad trick of standing in front of the fire, and so I burn my dresses," Jo said. "I scorched this one, so Meg told me to keep still so no one would see it. You may laugh, if you want to. It is funny, I know."

But Laurie didn't laugh. He only looked down a minute. The expression on his face puzzled Jo when he said very gently, "Never mind that. I'll tell you how we can manage. There's a long hall out there. We can dance grandly, and no one will see us. Please come."

Jo thanked him and gladly took his hand, wishing she had two neat gloves when she saw the nice pearl-colored ones Laurie wore. The hall was empty, and they danced a grand polka. This delighted Jo, because it was full of swing and spring.

When the music stopped, they sat down on the stairs to get their breath. Laurie told Jo all about his travels and how he had learned the polka when he was in Germany. Jo began asking dozens of questions about Europe, but then Meg appeared in search of her sister. She beckoned, and Jo reluctantly followed her into a side room. Meg was on a sofa, holding her foot and looking pale.

"I've sprained my ankle," Meg said, rocking in pain. "That horrid high heel turned and I fell. I can hardly stand, it aches so. I don't know how I'm ever going to get home."

"I knew you'd hurt your feet with those silly shoes," said Jo, softly rubbing the poor ankle. "I'm sorry. But I don't see what you can do except get a carriage or stay here all night."

"I'll rest till Hannah comes, and then do the best I can," Meg said.

"I'll ask Laurie for help," said Jo, feeling relieved as the idea occurred to her.

"Mercy, no! Don't ask or tell anyone," Meg replied firmly. "I can't dance any more, but as soon as supper is over, watch for Hannah and tell me the minute she comes."

"They are going out to supper now. I'll stay with you. I'd rather," Jo said, peeking out at the crowds.

"No, dear, run along and bring me some coffee. I'm so tired I can't move." Meg leaned back against the sofa, looking very sorry for herself.

So Jo went blundering away to the dining room, which she found only after first going into a china closet and then opening the door of a room where old Mr. Gardiner was having a lovely nap.

Jo darted at the table to grab the coffee. She immediately spilled it all down herself, making the front of her dress as much of a mess as the back.

"Oh dear, how clumsy I am!" exclaimed Jo. She scrubbed at her dress with Meg's precious glove, staining that in coffee too.

"Can I help you?" said a friendly voice. And there was Laurie with a full coffee cup in one hand and a plate in the other.

"I was trying to get something for Meg, who is very tired," said Jo. "But someone shook me, and here I am in a nice state." She glanced dismally from the stained skirt to the coffee-colored glove.

"Too bad! I was looking for someone to give this to. May I take it to your sister?" Laurie asked politely.

"Oh, thank you! I'll show you where she is. I won't offer to take it myself, because I'd be certain to spill it all over one of us." Jo grimaced.

Jo led the way. Laurie drew up a little table, fetching more coffee for Jo, and a whole dish of chocolates. He was so kind and polite that even fussy Meg pronounced him a "nice boy."

They had a merry time eating chocolates and chatting away. They had just started playing a funny word game with a couple of other guests when Hannah appeared. Meg forgot about her sore foot and stood so fast that she was forced to catch hold of Jo and yelped with pain.

"Hush! Don't say anything," Meg whispered to Jo, adding aloud, "It's nothing. I turned my foot a little, that's all." She limped upstairs to put her coat on.

Hannah scolded Meg, who cried, and Jo had no idea how they were going to get Meg home. She ran down, found a servant, and asked if he could get her a carriage. But it happened to be a hired waiter who knew nothing about the neighborhood. Jo was looking around for help when Laurie, who had heard what she said, came up and offered his grandfather's carriage. It had just come for him, Laurie said.

"It's so early! You can't mean to go yet?" began Jo, relieved but hesitating to accept the offer.

"I always go early, I do, truly!" Laurie insisted. "Please let me take you home. It's on my way, as you know, and I think it's going to rain."

That settled it. Jo told Laurie of Meg's mishap and gratefully accepted. She rushed up to bring down the rest of the party. Hannah hated rain as much as a cat did, so she made no trouble. They soon rolled away in the luxurious carriage, feeling very festive and elegant.

"I had a capital time. Did you?" Jo asked Meg, rumpling up her hair and making herself comfortable.

"Yes, till I hurt myself," answered Meg. "Sallie's friend Annie Moffat took a fancy to me and asked me to come and spend a week with her when Sallie does. She is going in the spring when the opera comes, and it will be perfectly splendid if Marmee lets me go."

"I saw you dancing with the red-headed man I ran away from. Was he nice?" Jo asked.

"Oh, very! His hair is auburn, not red, and he was very polite." Meg smiled.

"He looked like a grasshopper in a fit when he did the new step," Jo said. "Laurie and I couldn't help laughing. Did you hear us?"

Poor Laurie turned very pink. "I must say that is a very pretty dress," he said to Meg, changing the subject. "Such lovely silk."

Meg was so pleased that she was distracted from Jo's bad manners, and the three of them chatted happily until they were at home. With many thanks, the girls said goodnight and crept in, hoping to disturb no one. But the instant their door creaked, two little nightcaps bobbed up, and two sleepy but eager voices cried out . . .

"Tell us about the party! Tell us about the party!"

Jo had saved some chocolates for Amy and Beth, and so they munched away, listening eagerly to all the details.

"I declare," said Meg, "it really makes me feel like a fine young lady to come home from the party in a carriage and sit in my dressing gown with a maid to wait on me." Jo was binding up her foot and brushing her hair.

"I don't believe fine young ladies enjoy themselves any more than we do," said Jo. "In spite of our burnt hair, old gowns, one glove apiece, and tight slippers that sprain our ankles when we are so silly to wear them."

5.

"What in the world are you going to do now, Jo?" asked Meg one snowy afternoon not long after the party. Her sister was tramping along the hall in rubber boots and an old coat, with a broom in one hand and a shovel in the other.

"Going out for exercise," answered Jo with a playful twinkle in her eyes.

"You've already had two long walks this morning!" said Meg. "It's so cold outside, I advise you to stay warm and dry by the fire like me." She shivered.

"I can't keep still all day, and as I'm not a cat, I don't like to doze by the fire," Jo replied. "I like adventures, and I'm going to find some."

With a shrug, Meg went back to toast her feet and read. Jo began to dig paths in the snow with great energy.

The garden where Jo worked separated the Marches' house from their next-door neighbor.

Both houses stood on the edge of the city in a place that was still country-like, with trees and lawns, large gardens and quiet streets.

A low hedge ran between the two houses. On one side was Jo's home—an old brown house, looking rather bare and shabby without the vines that covered the walls in summer and the masses of flowers in the garden. On the other side of the hedge was a stately stone mansion with well-kept grounds, a huge glass conservatory, and lovely things visible between the rich curtains.

But it seemed like a lonely, lifeless sort of house. Few people went in and out except Mr. Laurence and his grandson.

In Jo's imagination, this fine house seemed a kind of enchanted palace, full of splendors and delights that no one enjoyed. She had long wanted to see inside and to know the Laurence boy. Since the party, Jo had been more eager than ever and had planned many ways of making friends with him, but he had not been seen lately, and Jo began to think he had gone away.

That day, however, Jo spotted a pale face up in the window. She had seen Mr. Laurence drive off earlier, and she knew Laurie was home alone.

There he is, thought Jo. *Poor boy! All alone and sick this dismal day. It's a shame!* With that thought, Jo scooped up a handful of snow, shaped it into a perfect snowball, and sent it sailing toward Laurie's window. It hit the glass with a thump, and Jo took a moment to be proud of her good aim.

Laurie's head turned at once, his big eyes brightening and his mouth beginning to smile. Jo nodded and laughed and waved her broom as she called out, "How do you do? Are you sick?"

Laurie opened the window and croaked out as hoarsely as a raven, "Better, thank you. I've had a bad cold and been stuck inside all week."

"I'm sorry. What do you amuse yourself with?" Jo asked.

"Nothing. It's dull as tombs up here," Laurie groaned.

"Isn't there some nice girl who'd read and amuse you?" Jo suggested.

"Don't know any." Laurie shrugged.

"You know us," began Jo, then laughed and stopped.

"So I do! Will you come over, please?" cried Laurie.

"I'm not really a nice girl, but I'll come if Marmee will let me," said Jo. "I'll go and ask her."

With that, Jo marched into the house carrying her broom, wondering what they would all say to her.

Laurie was in a flutter of excitement at the idea of having company. He flew about to get ready, trying to tidy his messy room by stacking things in teetering piles.

Finally, the doorbell gave a loud ring, then a determined voice could be heard asking for "Mr. Laurie." A surprised-looking servant came running up to announce a young lady.

"All right, show her up. It's Miss Jo," said Laurie, going to the door of his little parlor to meet Jo. She appeared looking rosy and relaxed, with a covered dish in one hand and a basket carrying Beth's three kittens in the other.

"Here I am, bag and baggage," Jo said. "Marmee sent her love and was glad if I could do anything for you. Meg wanted me to bring some of her jelly—she makes it very nicely—and Beth thought her cats would be comforting. I knew you'd laugh at them, but I couldn't refuse, Beth was so anxious to do something."

It so happened that Beth's funny loan was just the thing—Laurie forgot to be shy when all three of the kittens started trying to climb over him at once.

"That looks too pretty to eat," he said, smiling with pleasure as Jo uncovered the dish and showed the jelly. Amy had decorated it with a garland of green leaves and scarlet flowers.

"It isn't anything really, only they all felt sorry you were sick and wanted to do something kind. Meg thought you could eat the jelly without hurting your sore throat. What a cozy room this is!"

"I'm sorry about the mess," Laurie said awkwardly.

"It's not mess," Jo said. She took in the piles of books, the ice skates thrust into the corner, the pack of cards laid out on a table as if halfway through a game. "I think it's perfect. Now, shall I read to you like I promised?"

"If you don't mind, I'd rather just talk," Laurie said, and smiled a bit shyly.

"Not a bit. I'll talk all day if you'll let me. Beth says I never know when to stop." Jo flopped into a big armchair, and Laurie sat across from her.

"Is Beth the rosy one who stays at home a lot and sometimes goes out with a little basket?" asked Laurie with interest.

"Yes, that's Beth. The sweetest girl in all the world." Jo smiled.

"The pretty one is Meg, and the curly-haired one is Amy, I believe?" Laurie said.

"How did you find that out?" Jo asked.

Laurie blushed. "I often hear you calling to one another. When I'm alone up here, I can't help looking over at your house. You always seem to be having such good times. I beg your pardon for being so rude, but sometimes you forget to put down the curtain at the window where the flowers are. And when the lamps are lighted, it's like looking at a picture to see the fire, and you all around the table with your mother. Her face is right opposite the window, and it looks so sweet behind the flowers, I can't help watching it. I haven't got any mother, you know." Laurie poked the fire to hide a little twitching of the lips that he could not control.

The lonely, hungry look in his eyes went straight to Jo's warm heart. Her face was very friendly and her sharp voice unusually gentle as she said, "We'll never draw that curtain again, and you can look as much as you like. But I just wish, instead of peeping, you'd come over and see us. Marmee is so splendid, she'd do you heaps of good, and Beth would sing to you if I begged her to. Amy would dance—that wouldn't take any begging,

I assure you. Meg and I would make you laugh over our funny stage shows, and we'd have jolly times. Wouldn't your grandpa let you?"

"I think he would, if your mother asked him," said Laurie. "He's very kind, even if he does not look so, and he lets me do what I like, pretty much, only he's afraid I might be a bother to strangers." He was brightening more and more.

"We're not strangers; we're neighbors," Jo said firmly. "We want to know you."

"You see, Grandpa lives among his books and doesn't mind much what happens outside. Mr. Brooke, my tutor, doesn't stay here, and I have no one to go about with me, so I just end up staying inside by myself." Laurie looked sad again.

"That's bad," Jo said. "You should make an effort and go visiting everywhere you are asked, then you'll have plenty of friends and pleasant places to go to."

There was a little pause. "Do you like your school?" Laurie asked, changing the subject.

"I don't go to school," answered Jo. "I'm a businessman . . . girl, I mean. I go to look after my great-aunt, and a dear, cross old soul she is, too."

Laurie opened his mouth to ask another question, but, remembering just in time that it wasn't good manners to be nosy, he shut it again and looked uncomfortable.

Jo liked his good manners, but she certainly didn't mind sharing all her stories. She gave him a lively description of Aunt March, her fat poodle, the parrot that talked Spanish, and the library, which Jo loved.

Laurie enjoyed that immensely. She then told the story about the prim old gentleman who came once to woo Aunt March, and in the middle of a fine speech, how the parrot had tweaked his wig off. Laurie lay back and laughed till the tears ran down his cheeks.

"Oh! That does me no end of good. Tell on, please," Laurie said. He took his face out of the sofa cushion, red and shining with amusement.

Jo did "tell on," happily—all about their plays and plans, their hopes and fears for Father, and the most interesting events of the little world in which the sisters lived. Then they got to talking about books. To Jo's delight, she found that Laurie loved them as much as she did and had read even more than herself.

"If you like books so much, come down and see our library. Grandfather is out, so you needn't be afraid," said Laurie, getting up.

"I'm not afraid of anything," returned Jo with a toss of the head.

"I don't believe you are!" exclaimed Laurie, looking at her with much admiration.

Laurie led the way from room to room, letting Jo stop to examine whatever struck her fancy. At last they came to the library, where she clapped her hands and pranced, as she always did when she was especially happy. It was lined with books, and there were pictures and statues, and distracting little cabinets full of coins and curiosities. Big armchairs stood about and, best of all, there was a great open fireplace with tiles all round it.

"What richness!" sighed Jo. She sank into the depths of a chair and gazed about her contentedly. "Theodore Laurence, you should be the happiest boy in the world," she added.

"A fellow can't live on books," said Laurie, shaking his head as he perched on a table opposite.

Before he could say more, a bell rang. Jo flew up, exclaiming with alarm, "Mercy me! It must be your grandpa!"

"Well, what if it is? You are not afraid of anything, you know," said Laurie with a grin.

A maid appeared at the door. "The doctor to see you, sir," she said.

"Would you mind if I left you for a minute? I suppose I must see him," said Laurie.

"Don't mind me. I'm happy as a cricket here," answered Jo.

Laurie went away, and Jo wandered around the room again. She was standing before a fine portrait of Mr. Laurence when she heard the door open. Without turning, she said, "You know, Laurie, I'm sure now that I wouldn't be afraid of your grandfather, because he's got kind eyes, though his mouth is grim. He looks as if he has a tremendous will of his own. He isn't as handsome as my grandfather, but I like him."

"Thank you, ma'am," said a gruff voice behind her. Jo spun round, horrified to see that it was not Laurie who had come in at all but Mr. Laurence himself.

Poor Jo blushed till she couldn't blush any redder, and her heart began to beat uncomfortably fast as she thought about what she had said. She was gripped by a wild desire to run away, but that was cowardly, so she decided to stay and get out of the scrape as best she could.

A second look showed her that Mr. Laurence's eyes, under the bushy eyebrows, were kinder even than the ones in the painting, and there was a sly twinkle in them.

"So you're not afraid of me, eh?" Mr. Laurence asked.

"Not much, sir," Jo managed to reply.

"And you don't think me as handsome as your grandfather?" Mr. Laurence lifted his eyebrows.

"Not quite, sir." Jo began to smile.

"And I've got a tremendous will, have I?" Mr. Laurence asked.

"I only said I thought so," Jo pointed out.

"But you like me in spite of it?" Mr. Laurence said.

"Yes, I do, sir." Jo's smile grew.

That answer pleased the old gentleman. He gave a short laugh and shook hands with her. Putting his finger under Jo's chin, he turned up her face, examined it gravely and let it go, saying with a nod, "You've got your grandfather's spirit, even if you haven't got his face. He was a fine man, my dear, but what is better, he was a brave and an honest one. I was proud to be his friend."

"Thank you, sir," Jo said, feeling comfortable after that.

"What have you been doing to this boy of mine, eh?" was Mr. Laurence's next question.

"Only trying to be neighborly, sir." Jo told him how her visit came about.

"You think he needs cheering up a bit, do you?" Mr. Laurence asked.

"Yes, sir, he seems a little lonely. Young folks would do him good perhaps," Jo replied.

"There's the tea bell," Mr. Laurence said as a bell rang. "Come down with me and carry on being neighborly."

"If you'd like to have me, sir," Jo said.

"I wouldn't ask you if I didn't," Mr. Laurence said, offering her his arm.

What would Meg say to this? thought Jo as she was marched away, her eyes dancing with fun as she imagined herself telling the story at home.

6.

Soon the March girls had all made their way over to Laurie's house at one time or another. At first they were all a bit frightened of Mr. Laurence. But soon he had said something funny or kind to each one of them and talked over old times with their mother. Then nobody felt much afraid of him, except timid Beth.

The new friendship between the Marches and the Laurences flourished like grass in spring. Everyone liked Laurie, and he informed his tutor, Mr. Brooke, that the Marches were "regularly splendid girls."

What good times they had, to be sure. They put on plays, had sleigh rides and ice-skating frolics, and spent pleasant evenings in the old parlor. Now and then they all slipped next door for little parties at the great house.

Meg could walk in the Laurences' conservatory whenever she liked and enjoy the flowers, while Jo spent hours in the library. Amy copied pictures and enjoyed beauty to her heart's content, and Laurie played "lord of the manor" in the most delightful style.

But Beth had only gone once with Jo, and Mr. Laurence had stared at her so hard from under his heavy eyebrows that he frightened her, and she ran away. She'd declared she would never go there anymore, not even for the dear piano that she yearned to play.

Eventually Mr. Laurence learned about this, and he decided he would find a way to mend it. He called around to the March house and artfully led the conversation to music. He talked away about great singers he had seen and what fine organs he had heard, and told such charming stories. Soon Beth found it impossible to stay in her distant corner but crept nearer and nearer, as if fascinated.

She stopped at the back of his chair and stood listening, with her great eyes wide open and her cheeks red with excitement. Mr. Laurence talked on about Laurie's music lessons and teachers. And then, as if the idea had just occurred to him, he said to Marmee, "My grandson neglects his music now, and the piano suffers because no one plays it. Would some of your girls like to run over and practice on it now and then, just to keep it in tune?"

Beth took a step forward and pressed her hands tightly together to keep from clapping them.

Mr. Laurence went on with an odd little nod and smile, "They needn't see or speak to anyone but run in at any time. I'll be shut up in my study at the other end of the house, Laurie is out a great deal, and the servants are never near the drawing room after nine o'clock."

Mr. Laurence rose and added, "Please tell the young ladies what I say, and if they don't care to come, why, never mind."

Beth's little hand slipped into his, and she looked up at him with a face full of gratitude as she said, in her earnest yet timid way, "Oh, sir, they do care—very, very much!"

"Are you the musical girl?" Mr. Laurence asked as he looked down at her very kindly.

"I'm Beth. I love music dearly, and I'll come if you are quite sure nobody will hear me and be disturbed." She trembled at her own boldness as she spoke.

"Not a soul, my dear," Mr. Laurence said. "The house is empty half the day, so come and drum away as much as you like."

"How kind you are, sir!"

Beth blushed like a rose under the friendly look he wore, but she was not frightened now. She gave his hand a grateful squeeze because she had no words to thank him for the precious gift he had given her.

The old gentleman softly stroked the hair off her forehead. Stooping down, he said, "I had a little granddaughter once, with eyes like these. God bless you, my dear!" And away Mr. Laurence went in a great hurry.

Beth was delighted. How cheerfully she sang that evening, and how they all laughed at her because she woke Amy in the night by playing the piano on her face in her sleep.

The next day, Beth watched both Laurie and his grandfather leave. Then, after two or three retreats, she got in at the side door and made her way as noiselessly as any mouse to the drawing room.

Some pretty, easy music lay on the piano, quite by accident, of course. With trembling fingers and frequent stops to listen and look about, Beth at last touched the great instrument. Straightaway she forgot her fear, herself, and everything else but the unspeakable delight that the music gave her.

Beth stayed until Hannah came to take her home to dinner, but she had no appetite and could only sit and smile at everyone.

After that, Beth's little brown hood slipped through the hedge nearly every day, and the great drawing room was haunted by a tuneful spirit that came and went unseen. Beth never knew that Mr. Laurence opened his study door to hear the songs she played. She never saw Laurie guard the hall to warn the servants away. She never suspected that the exercise books and new songs that she found in the rack were put there for her.

"Marmee, I'm going to make Mr. Laurence a pair of slippers," said Beth one night. "He is so kind to me, I must thank him, and I don't know any other way. Can I do it?"

"Yes, dear. It will please him very much and be a nice way of thanking him," Marmee said.

After many serious discussions with Meg and Jo, the pattern was chosen, the materials bought, and the slippers begun. The design Beth chose was a group of pansies on a deeper purple background. She worked very hard on them, finishing them in record time. Then she wrote a short, simple note and, with Laurie's help, got them smuggled onto the study table one morning before Mr. Laurence was up.

When this excitement was over, Beth waited to see what would happen. All day passed and a part of the next, and she was beginning to fear she had offended her grumpy friend.

On the afternoon of the second day, Beth went out to do an errand. As she came up the street on her return, several joyful voices screamed, "Here's a letter from Mr. Laurence! Come quick and read it!"

"Oh, Beth, he's sent you—" began Amy, but she got no further for Jo slammed down the window.

Beth hurried to the house. At the door, her sisters dragged her to the parlor, all pointing and all saying at once, "Look there! Look there!"

Beth did look and turned pale with delight and surprise. There stood a little cabinet piano with a letter lying on the glossy lid to "Miss Elizabeth March."

"For me?" gasped Beth. She held on to Jo, feeling as if she would tumble down.

"Yes, all for you, my precious!" cried Jo. "Isn't it splendid of him? Don't you think he's the dearest old man in the world? Here's the key in the letter. We didn't open it, but we are dying to know what he says." She hugged her sister and offered the note.

"You read it! I can't! Oh, it is too lovely!" and Beth hid her face in Jo's apron, all upset by her present.

Jo opened the paper and began to laugh, for the first words she saw were "Dear Madam—"

"How nice it sounds! I wish someone would write to me like that!" said Amy, who thought the old-fashioned address very elegant.

"'I have had many pairs of slippers in my life, but I never had any that suited me so well as yours,'" continued Jo as she read the letter from Mr. Laurence. "'Pansies are my favorite flower, and these will always remind me of the gentle giver. I hope you will allow 'the old gentleman' to send you something that once belonged to the little granddaughter he lost. With hearty thanks and best wishes, I remain your grateful friend and humble servant, JAMES LAURENCE.'"

"There, Beth, that's an honor to be proud of, I'm sure!" said Jo, trying to soothe Beth, who trembled and looked more excited than she had ever been before.

"See the brackets to hold candles?" said Meg. "And the nice green silk, puckered up, with a gold rose in the middle, and the pretty rack and stool, all complete." She opened the instrument and displayed its beauties.

"'Your humble servant, James Laurence,'" said Amy. "Only think of his writing that to you. I'll tell the girls at school. They'll think it's splendid."

"Try it, honey," said Hannah, who always shared in the family joys and sorrows.

So Beth tried it, and everyone pronounced it the most remarkable piano ever heard.

"You'll have to go and thank him," said Jo as a joke, for the idea that Beth would really go never entered her head.

"Yes, I mean to. I guess I'll go now, before I get frightened thinking about it." And, to the utter amazement of her family, Beth walked down the garden, through the hedge, and in at the Laurences' door.

The girls were left quite speechless by the miracle.

They would have been still more amazed if they had seen what Beth did afterward. She went and knocked at the study door before she gave herself time to think.

When a gruff voice called out, "Come in!" she did go in, right up to Mr. Laurence, who looked quite taken aback.

Beth held out her hand, saying, with only a small quaver in her voice, "I came to thank you, sir, for . . ." But she didn't finish, for he looked so friendly that she forgot her speech, only remembering that he had lost the little girl he loved. So she put both arms round his neck and kissed him.

If the roof of the house had suddenly flown off, Mr. Laurence wouldn't have been more surprised. But he liked it. Beth stopped fearing him from that moment and sat there talking to him as cozily as if she had known him all her life. When she went home, Mr. Laurence walked with her to her own gate, shook hands cordially, and touched his hat. Then he marched back again, looking very stately and straight-backed, like a handsome, soldierly old gentleman, as he was.

When the girls saw that performance, Jo began to dance a jig and Amy nearly fell out of the window in her surprise. Meg exclaimed, with uplifted hands, "Well, I do believe the world is coming to an end."

7.

"Girls, where are you going?" asked Amy. She'd come into Jo and Meg's room one Saturday afternoon and found them getting ready to go out.

"Never mind. Little girls shouldn't ask questions," Jo replied sharply.

Meg never refused Amy anything for very long, so Amy turned to her. "Do tell me! I should think you might let me go too, because Beth is fussing over her piano, and I haven't got anything to do and am so lonely."

"I can't, dear, because you aren't invited," began Meg.

Jo broke in impatiently, "Now, Meg, be quiet or you will spoil it all. You can't go, Amy, so don't be a baby and whine about it."

"You are going somewhere with Laurie, I know you are," Amy said. "You were whispering and laughing together on the sofa last night, and you stopped when I came in. Aren't you going with him?"

"Yes, we are. Now do be still and stop bothering," Jo said.

"I know! I know! You're going to the theater to see the *Seven Castles*!" Amy cried. "I will go too, because Marmee said I might see it, and I've got my pocket money."

"Just listen to me a minute and be a good child," said Meg soothingly. "Marmee doesn't want you to go this week because you've had that horrid cold. Next week you can go with Beth and Hannah and have a nice time."

"I don't want to go with them. I want to go with you. Please let me. I've been sick with this cold so long, and I'm dying for some fun. Do, Meg! I'll be ever so good, and I'll pay for my own seat."

"You can't sit with us because our seats are reserved," Jo explained. "And you mustn't sit alone, so Laurie will give you his place, and that will spoil our fun. You just stay where you are."

Sitting on the floor with one boot on, Amy began to cry, and Meg tried to reason with her. When Laurie called from below, the two girls hurried down, leaving their sister wailing.

Just as the party was setting out, Amy called over the banisters, "You'll be sorry for this, Jo March."

"Fiddlesticks!" Jo replied, slamming the door.

They had a charming time, because the play was as brilliant and wonderful as a heart could wish, full of comical imps, sparkling elves, and gorgeous princes and princesses.

When they got home, they found Amy reading in the parlor. She never lifted her eyes from her book as they came in nor asked a single question.

The next day Jo made a terrible discovery.

Meg, Beth, and Amy were sitting together, late in the afternoon. Jo burst into the room looking excited and demanding breathlessly, "Has anyone taken my notebook?"

Meg and Beth said, "No," at once, and looked surprised. Amy poked the fire and said nothing.

"Amy, you've got it!" Jo exclaimed.

"No, I haven't," Amy replied.

"You know where it is, then!" Jo accused.

"No, I don't." Amy hid a small smile.

"That's a fib!" cried Jo. She took Amy by the shoulders, looking fierce enough to frighten a much braver child than Amy.

"It isn't. I haven't got it, don't know where it is now, and don't care," Amy said, her voice a bit squeaky. "Scold as much as you like, you'll never see your silly old book again."

Jo's eyes widened. "Why not?" she demanded.

Amy crossed her arms smugly. "I burned it up."

All the color left Jo's face, and Meg and Beth both gasped.

"What?" Jo exclaimed. "I worked so hard on my stories in my little book! I meant to finish before Father got home. Have you really burned it?"

"Yes, I did!" Amy said. "I told you I'd make you pay for being so cross yesterday, and I have, so—"

Amy got no further because Jo gripped her by the shoulders. "You wicked, wicked girl! I never can write it again, and I'll never forgive you as long as I live." With that, Jo turned and ran upstairs so that she could lose her temper in private.

There was a stunned silence in the parlor. Amy couldn't help noticing that Meg and Beth were looking at her as if she had done something really awful. But really, Jo deserved it . . . didn't she?

When Marmee came home and heard the story, she looked so sad and serious that Amy's stomach began to churn. Jo's book was the pride of her heart and was regarded by her family as holding great literary promise. It was only half a dozen little fairy tales, but Jo had worked over them patiently, putting her whole heart into her work, hoping to make something good enough to print.

When Marmee explained it that way, Amy began to see she had acted too hastily. In fact she was feeling very guilty indeed. Even soft-hearted Beth could hardly look at her.

When the tea bell rang, Jo appeared, looking grim and furious. It took all Amy's courage to say meekly, "Please forgive me, Jo. I'm very, very sorry."

"I will never forgive you" was Jo's stern answer, and from that moment she ignored Amy entirely.

As Jo received her goodnight kiss, Marmee whispered gently, "My dear, don't let the sun go down upon your anger. Forgive each other, help each other, and begin again tomorrow."

Jo wanted to lay her head down and cry her grief and anger all away, but she felt so deeply hurt that she really couldn't forgive Amy yet. So she blinked hard, shook her head, and said gruffly because Amy was listening, "It was an abominable thing, and she doesn't deserve to be forgiven."

8.

Jo's fury toward Amy continued for several days and may have lasted even longer had it not been for a dramatic turn of events.

Jo was still in a terrible mood, and the fact that her sisters and Marmee all kept urging her to forgive Amy only made matters worse. How could she possibly forgive something so terrible?

"Everybody is so hateful, I'll ask Laurie to go ice skating," said Jo to herself. "He is always kind and jolly, and will make me feel better, I know."

Amy heard the clash of skates and looked out the window, feeling annoyed.

"Jo promised I could go skating with her next time because this is the last ice we'll have," Amy exclaimed. "But it's no use to ask her to take me when she's being so mean to me."

"Don't say that," Meg replied. "You were very naughty, and it is hard to forgive the loss of her precious little notebook. But I think she might do it now, if you try her at the right minute. Go after them and apologize again."

"I'll try," said Amy. She got ready in a flurry and ran after the friends, who were just disappearing over the hill.

It wasn't far to the river. Jo saw Amy coming and turned her back, pretending not to. Laurie did not see because he was carefully skating along the shore, checking that the ice was safe.

"I'll go on to the first bend and see if it's all right before we begin to race" Amy heard Laurie say. He shot away in his fur-trimmed coat and cap.

Jo heard Amy panting behind her, but Jo never turned. Instead she went slowly zigzagging down the river, taking a bitter, unhappy sort of satisfaction in her sister's troubles.

As Laurie turned the bend, he shouted behind, "Keep near the shore. It isn't safe in the middle."

Jo heard him, but Amy did not catch a word.

Laurie had vanished around the bend, Jo not far behind him. Amy at the back began striking out toward the smoother ice in the middle of the river.

For a minute Jo paused with a strange feeling in her heart, then she decided to go on, but something held her and turned her round. She was just in time to see Amy throw up her hands and go down with a sudden crash of rotten ice, a splash of water, and a cry that made Jo's heart stand still with fear.

Jo tried to call Laurie, but her voice was gone. She tried to rush forward, but her feet seemed to have no strength in them. For a second she could only stand motionless, staring with terror at the little blue hood above the black water.

Something rushed swiftly by her, and Laurie's voice cried out, "Bring something for her to grab. Quick, quick!"

How she did it, Jo never knew, but for the next few minutes she worked as if possessed by someone else, blindly obeying Laurie, who was quite calm. Lying flat, Laurie held Amy up by his arm and hockey stick till Jo dragged a rail from the fence. Together they got the child out, who was more frightened than hurt.

"Now then, we must walk her home as fast as we can," cried Laurie. "Pile our things on her, while I get these skates off." He wrapped his coat around Amy and tugged away at the skate straps that had never seemed so intricate before.

They got Amy home, shivering, dripping, and crying. After an exciting time of it, she fell asleep, rolled in blankets before a hot fire.

During the bustle, Jo had hardly spoken but had flown about, looking pale and wild. Her things were half off, her dress torn, and her hands cut and bruised by the ice on the rail she had held.

When Amy was comfortably asleep and the house quiet, Mrs. March called Jo to her as she sat by Amy's bed and began to bind up Jo's hurt hands.

"Are you sure she is safe?" whispered Jo, looking with regret at the golden head. It might have been swept away from her sight forever under the dangerous ice.

"Quite safe, dear," her mother replied. "She is not hurt and won't even take cold, I think. You were so sensible in covering her and getting her home quickly."

"Laurie did it all. I only let her go. Marmee, if Amy should die, it would be my fault." And Jo dropped down beside the bed and burst into tears. "I was so angry, I didn't look after her properly. I didn't stop her from skating onto the unsafe ice."

Marmee stroked Jo's hair away from her face. "My poor Jo," Marmee said. "You've got a terrible temper just like mine, and it does make it very hard to forgive people."

"Marmee, you don't have a terrible temper!" Jo exclaimed.

Marmee nodded. "Oh, but I do," she said. "I have just learned over the years to control it better, and learned that you never know what is going to happen. It's important to forgive the people you love just as soon as you can."

Jo was quiet, thinking over her mother's words. "I have felt worse and worse the longer I've stayed angry," Jo admitted finally. "It was harder and harder to forgive Amy the longer it went on."

"What Amy did was very cruel," Marmee said. "We all know what that book meant to you and how hard you had worked on it, but she regretted it terribly. I think you have to realize that Amy shares our bad temper as well. We must all help each other to overcome it."

Amy stirred then and opened her eyes, blinking up at her sister.

"Marmee is right, Jo," Amy said softly. "I'm so sorry for hurting you and burning your dear old book. Please forgive me?"

"Of course I forgive you," Jo said, her voice a bit wobbly. "If you'll forgive me and promise we'll try to overcome our hasty tempers together?"

Amy held out her arms with a smile that went straight to Jo's heart. They didn't say a word but hugged one another close, in spite of the blankets, and everything was forgiven and forgotten in one hearty kiss.

9.

As spring came on, a new set of amusements became the fashion. This included the garden, which had to be put in order, and each sister had a quarter of the little plot to do what she liked with.

Meg's bit of garden was full of roses, with a small orange tree in it. Jo's flower beds were never alike from season to season because she was always trying experiments. This year it was to be towering, cheerful sunflowers. Beth had old-fashioned fragrant flowers in her garden—sweet peas and larkspur, pinks, pansies, wildflowers for the bees. Amy had put a small, pretty arch in her garden, with honeysuckle in graceful wreaths all over it, as well as tall white lilies and delicate ferns.

Gardening, walks, rowing boats on the river, and flower hunts kept them busy over the fine days. For rainy ones they had other activities to look forward to.

One of these was called the "P.C.," which was short for the Pickwick Club. (A name the girls had chosen because they were big fans of Charles Dickens.)

The Pickwick Club met every Saturday in the big attic. Three chairs were arranged in a row in front of a table on which was a lamp and four white badges with a big "P.C." in different colors on each.

There was also the weekly newspaper called *The Pickwick Portfolio*, which Jo made as the editor. All four girls wrote stories, reviews, poems, advertisements, and even recipes that were featured in *The Pickwick Portfolio*.

At seven o'clock, the four members arrived, put their badges on, and took their seats with great seriousness. Meg's name in the group was Samuel Pickwick, Jo was called Augustus Snodgrass, Beth was known as Tracy Tupman, and Amy was Nathaniel Winkle.

Meg was the president and usually read the paper aloud while all the girls had a cosy time laughing over the week's tales.

On this occasion, Meg as Mr. Pickwick put on a pair of spectacles without any glass in them and rapped upon the table. "I believe Mr. Snodgrass wishes to make an announcement this week," she said, looking at Jo.

Jo got to her feet, adjusting the rather battered top hat that perched on her head.

"Mr. President and gentlemen," Jo began, as if she were speaking in a parliament, "I wish to propose the admission of a new member—one who highly deserves the honor, would be deeply grateful for it, and would be jolly and nice. I propose Mr. Theodore Laurence as an honorary member of the P.C. Come now, do have him."

Jo's sudden change of tone made the girls laugh, but all of them looked rather worried, and no one said a word.

"We'll put it to a vote," said Meg. "All in favor of this motion, say 'Aye.'"

There was a loud response from Jo, followed by a timid one from Beth, to everybody's surprise.

Meg and Amy were both silent.

Amy rose with great elegance. "We don't wish for any boys," she said. "They only joke and bounce about. This is a ladies' club, and we wish to be private and proper."

"I'm afraid Laurie will laugh at our paper and make fun of us afterward," said Meg unhappily.

Jo jumped to her feet. "Sir, I give you my word that, as a gentleman, Laurie won't do anything of the sort. He likes to write, and he'll enjoy himself. We can do so little for him, and he does so much for us. So I think the least we can do is to offer him a place here and make him welcome if he comes."

Beth surprised the group again by leaping to her feet. "Yes, we really should let him, even if we are afraid. I say he may come." Here, Beth's voice got even louder, her eyes burning. "And his grandpa can come too if he likes!"

This spirited burst electrified the club, and Jo left her seat to shake hands with Beth approvingly.

"Now then, let's vote again. Everybody remember it's our Laurie and say 'Aye!'" cried Jo excitedly.

"Aye! Aye! Aye!" replied three voices at once.

"Good! Now, allow me to present the new member." And to the dismay of the rest of the club, Jo threw open the door of the closet. Inside, Laurie was sitting on a rag bag, flushed and twinkling with suppressed laughter.

"You rogue! You traitor! Jo, how could you?" cried the other three girls as Jo led her friend triumphantly forth. She produced both a chair and a badge, and had him settled in nicely in a jiffy.

"The coolness of you two rascals is amazing," said Meg. She tried to frown an awful frown but only succeeded in producing a friendly smile.

Laurie rose smoothly to his feet and said, "Mr. President and ladies—I beg pardon, gentlemen— allow me to introduce myself as Sam Weller, the very humble servant of the club."

"Good! Good!" cried Jo, pounding the floor with the handle of the old warming pan she'd been leaning on.

Laurie continued, with a wave of the hand, "My faithful friend and noble patron, who has so flatteringly presented me, is not to be blamed for me being here. I planned it, and Jo only gave in after lots of teasing."

"Come now, don't lay it all on yourself. You know the cupboard was my idea," broke in Jo, who was enjoying the joke hugely.

"Never mind what she says. I'm the wretch who did it, sir," said the new member. "But on my honor, I never will do so again. I henceforth devote myself to the interest of this immortal club."

"Hear! Hear!" cried Jo, clashing the lid of the warming pan like a cymbal.

Laurie's smile grew wider. "As a token of my gratitude, I have set up a post office in the hedge in the lower corner of the garden. It's a big old bird house, but I've stopped up the door and made the roof open so it will hold all sorts of things and save our valuable time. Letters, manuscripts, books, and bundles can be passed in there. Allow me to present the club key."

With that, Laurie placed a shiny little key on the table. There was a great round of applause, the warming pan clashed and waved wildly, and it was some time before order could be restored. The meeting finally broke up with three shrill cheers for the new member.

10.

The P.O. (as they all called the new post office) flourished wonderfully. Almost as many interesting things passed through it as through the real post office. Handwritten stories and bowties, poetry and pickles, garden seeds and long letters, music and gingerbread. All of these things were left in the bird house.

Old Mr. Laurence liked the fun and amused himself by sending odd bundles, mysterious messages, and funny telegrams. His gardener, who was smitten with Hannah's charms, actually sent a love letter to her, care of Jo. How they laughed when the secret came out, never dreaming how many love letters that little post office would hold in the years to come.

Beth was in charge of the P.O. because she was at home the most, and she loved the daily task of unlocking the little door and handing out the mail. One day she came in with her hands full and went about the house leaving letters and parcels like the penny post.

"Here are your flowers, Marmee! Laurie never forgets them," Beth said, putting the fresh bouquet in the vase that stood in "Marmee's corner."

"Miss Meg March, one letter and a glove," continued Beth, delivering the articles to her sister, who sat stitching an old skirt.

"How strange," said Meg, looking at the gray cotton glove. "I lost a pair the other day but here's only one of them turned up." She frowned. "I do hate to have odd gloves! Never mind, the other may be found."

"Who is the letter from?" Beth asked.

"It's a translation of the German song I wanted," Meg said, smiling as she read the words. "I think Laurie's tutor, Mr. Brooke, did it, because this isn't Laurie's writing."

"Two letters for Jo, a book, and a funny old hat, which was on top of the post office, covering the whole thing," said Beth, laughing as she went into the study, where Jo sat writing.

"What a sly fellow Laurie is!" Jo grinned. "I said I wished bigger hats were the fashion because I burn my face every hot day. He said, 'Why mind the fashion? Wear a big hat and be comfortable!'

I said I would if I had one, and he has sent me this to try me. I'll wear it for fun and show him I don't care for fashion."

As it happened, Jo bumped into Laurie the next day. Autumn was coming in now, and the air had a bit of a chill to it. The leaves were just beginning to turn.

Laurie was out for a walk when he spied Jo stomping along the road, coming from the direction of the town.

"Jo!" Laurie called, and Jo looked up. At once, Laurie knew that something was up because Jo was frowning anxiously. But quickly her expression changed to a smile.

"Hello, Laurie!" Jo said, and he fell into step beside her.

"May I walk with you and tell you something very interesting?" Laurie said.

"Of course," Jo said. "I always like to hear interesting things."

"Very well then, come on," Laurie replied. "It's a secret, and if I tell you, you must tell me yours."

"I haven't got any secrets," began Jo, but stopped suddenly, as if remembering that she had.

"You know you have—you can't hide anything, and I can see it all over your face, so you tell me yours and I'll tell you mine," cried Laurie.

"Is your secret a nice one?" Jo asked with suspicion.

"Oh, yes!" Laurie insisted. "All about people you know, and such fun! You should hear it, and I've been aching to tell it this long time. Come, you begin."

"You'll not say anything about it at home, will you?" Jo asked.

"Not a word," Laurie promised. "Fire away."

"Well, I've left two of my short stories at the newspaper, and they're going to let me know next week if they'll print them," whispered Jo.

"Hurrah for Miss March, the celebrated American authoress!" cried Laurie. He threw up his hat and caught it again, to the great delight of two ducks, four cats, and five hens.

"Hush! It won't come to anything, I daresay, but I couldn't rest till I had tried, and I said nothing about it because I didn't want anyone else to be disappointed." Jo shrugged.

"It won't fail. Why, Jo, your stories are works of Shakespeare compared to half the rubbish that is published every day. Won't it be fun to see them in print, and shall we not feel proud of you?" Laurie rubbed his hands together.

Jo's eyes sparkled. "Now, what's your secret?" she asked. "Play fair, Laurie, or I'll never believe you again."

"I may get into a scrape for telling you," Laurie said. "But I didn't promise not to, so I will, because I never feel easy in my mind till I've told you any exciting bit of news I get. I know where Meg's glove is." A smile pulled at his mouth.

"Is that all?" said Jo, looking disappointed.

"It's quite enough for now, as you'll agree when I tell you where it is," Laurie smirked.

"Tell me then," Jo insisted.

Laurie bent forward and whispered, "My tutor, Mr. Brooke, has it."

Jo stood and stared at Laurie for a minute, looking both surprised and displeased. Then she walked on, saying sharply, "How do you know?"

"I saw it," Laurie said.

"Where?" Jo demanded.

"In his pocket," Laurie replied.

Jo frowned. "All this time?"

"Yes, I think he's in love with her. Isn't that romantic?" Laurie batted his eyelashes.

"No, it's horrid." Jo stomped off ahead.

"I thought you'd be pleased," Laurie said, catching up with Jo easily.

"At the idea of anybody coming to take Meg away? No, thank you." Jo stuffed her hands in her pockets.

"You'll feel better about it when somebody comes to take you away," Laurie said.

"I'd like to see anyone try it," cried Jo fiercely.

"So should I!" Laurie chuckled at the idea.

"I don't think secrets agree with me. I feel rumpled up in my mind now," said Jo rather ungratefully.

"Race down this hill with me, and you'll be all right," suggested Laurie.

No one was in sight, and the smooth road sloped invitingly before her. Finding the temptation irresistible, Jo darted away, soon leaving hat and comb behind her and scattering hairpins as she ran. Laurie won the race, but Jo's face was brighter, and he politely offered to go back and pick up all the things she had dropped on the way down.

Jo bundled up her braids, hoping no one would pass by till she was tidy again. But someone did pass, and who should it be but Meg, looking particularly ladylike.

"What in the world are you doing here?" Meg asked Jo.

"Getting leaves," Jo replied quietly, sorting the rosy handful she had just swept up.

"And hairpins," added Laurie, throwing half a dozen into Jo's lap. "They grow on this road, Meg. So do combs and brown straw hats."

"You have been running, Jo," said Meg. "How could you? When will you stop such romping ways?"

"Never till I'm stiff and old. Don't try to make me grow up before my time, Meg. It's hard enough that you have changed all of a sudden. Let me be a little girl as long as I can."

There was a bit of a tremble in Jo's voice. It seemed to her lately that things were changing, and Meg was turning into a real young lady. Laurie's secret made Jo dread the future when she knew her sister would get married and leave their lovely, comfortable home.

Laurie saw how upset Jo was and drew Meg's attention from it by asking quickly, "Where have you been calling, dressed so nice?"

"At the Gardiners' house," Meg said. "Sallie has been telling me all about her friend's wedding. It was very splendid, and they have gone to spend the winter in Paris. Just think how delightful that must be!"

"Do you envy her, Meg?" said Laurie.

"I'm afraid I do," Meg replied.

"I'm glad of it!" muttered Jo, tying on her hat with a jerk.

"Why?" asked Meg, looking surprised.

"Because if you care so much about riches, you will never go and marry a poor man," said Jo.

"I shall never '*go* and marry' anyone," said Meg. She walked on with great dignity while Jo and Laurie followed, laughing, whispering, skipping stones, and "behaving like children," as Meg said to herself. Despite that, she might have been tempted to join them if she had not had her best dress on.

For a week or two after that, Jo behaved so oddly that her sisters were quite bewildered. Jo rushed to the door when the postman rang, was rude to Mr. Brooke whenever they met, and would sit looking at Meg with a sad face, sometimes jumping up to shake and then kiss her in a very mysterious manner. Laurie and Jo were always whispering secrets to one another.

One day, Jo bounced into the parlor with a newspaper in her hands. She laid herself on the sofa and began to shake the newspaper out noisily as if she were about to read it.

"Have you anything interesting there?" asked Meg.

"Nothing but a story, which won't amount to much, I guess," replied Jo.

"You'd better read it aloud. That will amuse us and keep you out of mischief," said Amy in her most grown-up tone.

"What's the name of the story?" asked Beth, wondering why Jo kept her face hidden behind the paper.

"The Rival Painters," Jo replied.

"That sounds interesting. Read it," said Meg.

With a loud "Ahem!" and a long breath, Jo began to read very fast. The girls listened with interest, because the tale was very romantic and quite sad, as most of the characters died in the end.

"I like that bit about the splendid picture," Amy commented as Jo paused.

"I prefer the romantic part," said Meg, wiping her eyes because it had been quite tragic. "Viola and Angelo are two of our favorite names—isn't that funny?"

"Who wrote it?" asked Beth.

Jo sat up and cast away the paper, showing off a very pink face. With a funny mixture of seriousness and excitement, she replied in a loud voice, "Your sister."

"You?" cried Meg.

"It's very good," said Amy.

"I knew it! I knew it!" Beth said. "Oh, my Jo, I am so proud!" She ran to hug her sister.

Dear me, how delighted they all were! Meg wouldn't really believe it until she saw the words "Miss Josephine March" actually printed in the paper.

Amy criticized the artistic parts of the story with sensitivity and offered hints for a sequel, which unfortunately couldn't be carried out as the hero and heroine were now dead. Beth got excited and skipped and sang with joy. Hannah came in to exclaim, "Sakes alive, well I never!" Marmee was extremely proud.

"Tell us about it." "When did it come?" "How much did you get for it?" "What will Father say?" "Won't Laurie laugh?" cried the family, all in one breath as they clustered about Jo.

"Stop jabbering, girls, and I'll tell you everything," said Jo. But then she took one look at the proud shining faces around her and hid her own in the newspaper for a good cry.

11.

"November is the most disagreeable month in the whole year," said Meg. She was standing at the window one dull afternoon, looking out at the frostbitten garden.

"That's the reason I was born in it," said Jo.

"If something very pleasant should happen now, we would think it a delightful month," said Beth, who took a hopeful view of everything, even November.

Meg only sighed.

Sitting at the other window, Beth said with a smile, "Two pleasant things are going to happen right away. Marmee is coming down the street, and Laurie is tramping through the garden for a visit."

In they both came, Marmee with her usual question: "Any letter from Father, girls?"

While Laurie said in his persuasive way, "Won't some of you come for a drive?"

"Of course we will," Jo answered Laurie.

"We can be ready in a minute," cried Amy, running away to wash her hands.

A sharp ring at the door interrupted them then, and a minute later Hannah came in with a letter.

"It's one of them horrid telegram things," Hannah said, handling it as if she was afraid it would explode.

At the word "telegram," Marmee snatched it, read the two lines it contained and dropped back into her chair. She was as white as if the little paper had sent a bullet to her heart. Laurie dashed downstairs for water, while Meg and Hannah supported her, and Jo read aloud, in a frightened voice:

Mrs. March

Your husband is very ill. Come at once.

S. Hale
Blank Hospital, Washington

The room was still as they listened breathlessly, the day strangely darkening outside. The girls gathered about their mother as the whole world seemed to change.

Marmee seemed to pull herself together and stretched out her arms to her daughters. "I will go at once," she said. "Come on, girls, and help me get ready. Where's Laurie?"

"Here I am. Oh, let me do something!" cried Laurie. He hurried in from the next room, where he had been hovering with the water he'd fetched, giving the family a moment of privacy.

"Send a telegram saying I will come at once," Marmee said. "The next train goes early in the morning. I'll take that."

"What else? The horses are ready. I can go anywhere, do anything," Laurie said, looking ready to fly to the ends of the earth.

"Leave a note at Aunt March's. Jo, give me that pen and paper."

Jo went to get the paper with a heavy heart. Marmee would be asking Aunt March for the money to make the journey to see Father. Jo wished she could help.

With the note in his hand, Laurie sped out of the room.

"Jo, I have a list of things I need you to go and buy," Marmee said. "Hospital stores are not always good. Beth, go and ask Mr. Laurence for a couple of bottles of old wine. I'm not too proud to beg for Father. He shall have the best of everything. Amy, tell Hannah to get down the black trunk, and Meg, come and help me find my things." Marmee gave her orders rapidly.

Everyone scattered like leaves before a gust of wind. The calm, happy household was broken up as suddenly as if the telegram had been an evil spell.

Mr. Laurence came hurrying back with Beth, bringing every comfort the kind old gentleman could think of for Mr. March. There was nothing he didn't offer, from his own dressing gown to himself as escort. But the last was impossible. Mrs. March would not hear of the old gentleman undertaking the long journey.

Meg ran through the hall with a pair of boots in one hand and a cup of tea in the other, and came suddenly upon Mr. Brooke.

"I'm very sorry to hear of this, Miss March," he said in his kind, quiet voice. His handsome face wore a worried expression. "I know Mr. Laurence can't accompany your mother to Washington, but I'd like to offer my services. I'm sure there are lots of things I can do to be useful, and Mr. Laurence has said I may go."

Meg dropped the boots to the floor, the tea very near following, as she put out her hand and grasped Mr. Brooke's fingers in her own.

"How kind you are! Marmee will accept, I'm sure, and it will be such a relief to know that she has someone to take care of her. Thank you very, very much!"

Everything was arranged by the time Laurie returned with a note from Aunt March, enclosing the sum Marmee had asked for. The short afternoon wore away, and soon all the other errands were completed. Meg and her mother were busy at some necessary needlework while Beth and Amy got tea, but still Jo did not come home from her errands.

They began to get anxious, and they were all very confused when Jo came rushing in, dropping a bundle of banknotes on the table. She said with a little choke in her voice, "That's my contribution toward making Father comfortable and bringing him home!"

"My dear, where did you get it? Twenty-five dollars!" Marmee exclaimed.

"I didn't beg, borrow, or steal it. I earned it, and I don't think you'll blame me, for I only sold what was my own," Jo said. As she spoke, Jo took off her bonnet, and a cry rang around the room because Jo's hair had all been cut off.

"Your hair! Your beautiful hair! Oh, Jo, how could you? Your one beauty," Meg exclaimed.

"She doesn't look like my Jo any more, but I love her dearly for it!" Beth said, hugging Jo tight.

"It doesn't affect the fate of the nation, so don't wail, Beth," Jo said. "It will do my brains good to have that mop taken off. My head feels deliciously light and cool, and the barber said I could soon have a curly crop, which will be boyish, becoming and easy to keep in order. I'm satisfied, so please take the money and let's have supper." She pretended not to mind losing her hair at all.

"What made you do it?" asked Amy, who would as soon have thought of cutting off her head as her pretty hair.

"Well, I was wild to do something for Father," replied Jo as they gathered about the table. "I hadn't the least idea of selling my hair at first, but as I went along I kept thinking what I could do. In a barber's window I saw some lovely wigs. It came to me all of a sudden that I had one thing to make money out of. Without stopping to think, I walked in, asked if they bought hair and what they would give for mine."

"I don't see how you dared to do it," said Beth in a tone of awe.

"Oh, the barber was very surprised. Said he wasn't used to having girls bounce into his shop and ask him to buy their hair. He said he didn't care about mine, it wasn't a fashionable color, and he never paid much for it in the first place. So I begged him to take it and told him why I was in such a hurry. It was silly, I dare say, but it changed his mind."

"Didn't you feel terrible when the first cut came?" asked Meg with a shiver.

"I took a last look at my hair while the man got his things, and that was the end of it," Jo said. "He picked out a long lock for me to keep. I'll give it to you, Marmee, just to remember past glories by, because having it short is so comfortable I don't think I'll ever have it long again." She still tried to look very unbothered.

Mrs. March folded the wavy chestnut lock and laid it together with a short gray one in her desk.

At ten o'clock Marmee said, "Come, girls. Go to bed and don't talk, for we must be up early and shall need all the sleep we can get."

Nobody wanted to go, but they kissed her quietly and went to bed. Beth and Amy soon fell asleep in spite of everything, but Meg lay awake, thinking the most serious thoughts she had ever known in her short life. Jo lay motionless, and Meg thought that she was asleep until she heard a little sob.

"Jo, dear, what is it? Are you crying about Father?" Meg asked.

"No, not now," Jo said sadly.

"What then?" Meg placed a hand on Jo's arm.

"My . . . my hair!" burst out poor Jo, trying to smother her emotion in the pillow.

Meg hugged the heroine tenderly.

"I'm not sorry," Jo explained with a choke. "I'd do it again tomorrow if I could. It's only the vain part of me that goes and cries in this silly way. Don't tell anyone. It's all over now. I thought you were asleep or I wouldn't have made a sound. Why are you awake?"

"I can't sleep, I'm so anxious," said Meg.

"Think about something pleasant, and you'll soon drop off," Jo said.

"I tried it but felt wider awake than ever."

"What did you think of?" Jo asked.

"Handsome faces—eyes particularly," answered Meg, smiling to herself in the dark.

12.

"Meg, I wish you'd go and see the Hummels," said Beth, ten days after Mrs. March's departure. "You know Marmee told us not to forget them."

"I'm too tired to go this afternoon," replied Meg, rocking comfortably as she sewed.

"Can't you go, Jo?" asked Beth.

"I don't feel well enough with my cold," Jo sniffled. She had caught a nasty cold the week before.

"I thought it was almost better," Beth said.

"It's well enough for me to go out with Laurie, but not well enough to go to the Hummels'," said Jo. She laughed but looked a little ashamed of herself.

"Why don't you go yourself?" Meg asked Beth.

"I have been every day, but the baby is sick, and I don't know what to do for it," Beth replied, twisting her hands. "I think you or Hannah should go."

"I promise I'll go tomorrow," Meg said. "Ask Hannah for some of that nice cake and take it to them, Beth. The air will do you good."

"My head aches and I'm tired, so I thought maybe some of you would go," said Beth.

"Amy will be back soon, and she will run down for us," suggested Meg.

So Beth lay down on the sofa, the others returned to their work, and the Hummels were forgotten.

An hour passed. Amy did not come, Meg went to her room to try on a new dress, and Jo was absorbed in her story. So Beth quietly put on her hood, filled her basket with odds and ends for the poor Hummel children, and went out into the chilly air.

It was late when Beth came back, and no one saw her creep upstairs and shut herself into Marmee's room. Half an hour later, Jo found Beth sitting on the medicine chest, looking very serious, with red eyes and a medicine bottle in her hand.

"What's the matter?" cried Jo.

Beth put out her hand as if to warn her off and asked, "You've had the scarlet fever, haven't you?"

"Years ago, when Meg did. Why?" Jo said.

"Then I'll tell you. Oh, Jo, the baby's dead!" Beth's voice shook.

"What baby?" Jo asked, bewildered.

"Mrs. Hummel's baby. It died in my arms," cried Beth with a sob.

"My poor dear, how dreadful for you! I should have gone," said Jo, taking her sister's hand.

"It was very sad, and I cried with them until the doctor came," Beth said. "He told them it was scarlet fever. Then he turned round all of a sudden and told me to go home and take some medicine right away or I'd be ill too."

"No, you won't!" cried Jo, hugging Beth close with a frightened look. "Oh, Beth, if you should be sick, I never could forgive myself! What shall we do?"

"Don't be frightened," said Beth. "I looked in Marmee's book and saw that it begins with a headache and a sore throat, which I do have, so I took some medicine. Now I feel better." She pressed her cold hands on her hot forehead and tried to look well.

"If only Marmee was at home!" exclaimed Jo. She seized the book, feeling that Washington was an immense way off. She read a page, looked at Beth, felt her head, and peeped into her throat. Then she said gravely, "You've been over with the baby every day for more than a week, so I'm afraid you are going to have it, Beth. I'll call Hannah—she knows all about sickness."

"Don't let Amy come," said Beth. "She never had it, and I should hate to give it to her. Are you sure you and Meg can't have it a second time?"

"I think not. Don't care if I do. It would serve me right, selfish pig, to let you go and stay writing rubbish myself!" Jo went to consult Hannah.

Hannah took the lead at once, assuring that there was no need to worry—everyone caught scarlet fever, and if rightly treated, nobody died. Jo believed it all and felt much relieved as they went up to call Meg.

"Now, I'll tell you what we'll do," said Hannah, after she had examined and questioned Beth. "We will have Dr. Bangs over, just to take a look at you, dear, and see that we start right. Then we'll send Amy off to Aunt March's for a spell, to keep her out of harm's way."

But Amy passionately declared that she would rather have the fever than go to Aunt March. Meg reasoned, pleaded, and commanded, but Amy protested that she would not go. Fortunately, Laurie arrived then and when he heard the news, he crouched down in front of Amy.

"Now be a sensible little woman and do as they say," Laurie said to Amy. "No, don't cry, but hear what a jolly plan I've got. You go to Aunt March's, and I'll come and take you out every day, driving or walking, and we'll have capital times. Won't that be better than moping here?"

"I don't wish to be sent off as if I was in the way," began Amy in a hurt voice.

"You don't want to be sick, do you?" Laurie asked, and Amy considered this.

"Will you take me out in the trotting wagon?" she asked.

"On my honor as a gentleman." Laurie put a hand on his heart.

"And come every single day?" Amy asked.

"See if I don't!" Laurie replied.

"And bring me back the minute Beth is well?" Amy demanded.

"The very minute," Laurie agreed.

"Well, I guess I will," said Amy slowly.

And so it was settled, and Meg and Jo were very grateful for Laurie's intervention.

"How is the little dear?" asked Laurie, because he was very fond of Beth, and he felt more anxious about her than he liked to show.

"She is lying down on Marmee's bed and feels better," Meg answered. "But Hannah looks worried, and that makes me fidgety."

"What a trying world it is!" said Jo, rumpling up her hair in a fretful way.

"Well, don't make a porcupine of yourself. It isn't becoming," Laurie said. "Should I telegraph your mother or do anything?"

"That is what troubles me," said Meg. "I think we should tell Marmee if Beth is really ill, but Hannah says we mustn't, for Marmee can't leave Father, and it will only make them anxious."

"You could ask Grandfather what he thinks after the doctor has been," Laurie suggested.

Dr. Bangs came and said Beth had symptoms of the fever, but he thought she would have it lightly. Amy was ordered off at once, and then there was nothing to do but wait and worry.

13.

Beth did have the fever and was much sicker than anyone but Hannah and the doctor suspected.

Jo devoted herself to Beth day and night. When the fever struck, Beth began to talk in a hoarse, broken voice, to play on the blanket as if on her beloved little piano, and tried to sing with a throat so swollen that there was no music left. She did not seem to know the familiar faces around her, and addressed them by wrong names, and called urgently for Marmee.

They received a letter from Washington that added to their trouble, because their father was still very ill and could not think of coming home for a long while.

How dark the days seemed now, how sad and lonely the house. The hearts of the sisters were heavy as they worked and waited while the shadow of death hovered over the once happy home.

Laurie haunted the house like a restless ghost, and Mr. Laurence locked the grand piano. Everyone missed Beth. The milkman, baker, grocer, and butcher asked how she did; the neighbors sent all sorts of comforts and good wishes. Even those who knew Beth best were surprised to find how many friends the shy little woman had made.

Dr. Bangs came twice a day, Hannah sat up at night, Meg kept a telegram in her desk all ready to send off to Washington at any minute, and Jo never stirred from Beth's side.

The first of December was a wintry day indeed to them, for a bitter wind blew and snow fell fast. When Dr. Bangs came that morning, he looked long at Beth, held her hot hand in both of his own for a minute, and laid it gently down. Then he said in a low voice to Hannah, "If Mrs. March can leave her husband, she'd better be sent for."

Hannah nodded without speaking. Meg dropped down into a chair as the strength seemed to go out of her limbs at the sound of those words. Jo stood with a pale face for a minute, then ran to the parlor and snatched up the telegram. Throwing on her things, she rushed out into the storm.

Jo was soon back, and while taking off her cloak, Laurie came in with a letter saying that

Mr. March was finally getting better. Jo read it thankfully, but the heavy weight did not seem lifted off her heart. Her face was so full of misery that Laurie asked quickly, "What is it? Is Beth worse?"

"I've sent for Marmee," said Jo. "The doctor told us to."

"Oh, Jo, it's not so bad as that?" cried Laurie with a startled face.

"Yes, it is." The tears streamed fast down poor Jo's cheeks and she stretched out her hand in a helpless sort of way, as if searching in the dark.

Laurie took her hand in his, whispering as well as he could with a lump in his throat, "I'm here. Hold on to me, Jo dear!"

Soon Jo dried her tears and looked up with a grateful face.

"Thank you, Laurie, I'm better now," she said.

"Keep hoping for the best—that will help you, Jo," Laurie said. "Soon your mother will be here, and then everything will be all right."

"You are a good friend, Laurie. How can I ever repay you?" Jo asked.

"I'll send my bill," Laurie joked, "and tonight I'll give you good news." He beamed at her.

"What is it?" Jo asked.

"I telegraphed to your mother yesterday, and Brooke answered she'd come at once. She'll be here tonight, and everything will be all right. Aren't you glad I did it?" Laurie spoke very fast and turned red. He had kept his plan a secret for fear of disappointing the girls or harming Beth.

Jo's face grew white, and she flew out of her chair. The moment he stopped speaking, she electrified him by throwing her arms round his neck and crying out joyfully, "Oh, Laurie! Oh, Marmee! I am so glad! Laurie, you're an angel! How shall I ever thank you?"

"Fly at me again. I rather liked it," said Laurie, looking playful, a thing he had not done for a fortnight.

A breath of fresh air seemed to blow through the house, and something better than sunshine brightened the quiet rooms. Everything appeared to feel the hopeful change. The fires seemed to burn with odd cheeriness, and every time the girls met, their pale faces broke into smiles as they hugged one another, whispering, "Marmee is coming!"

Worn out, Hannah lay down on the sofa at the bed's foot and fell fast asleep, while Mr. Laurence marched to and fro. Laurie lay on the rug, pretending to rest but staring into the fire with a thoughtful look that made his black eyes beautifully soft and clear.

Meg and Jo never forgot that night, sitting up by Beth's bed for hour after hour.

The house was as still as death, the only sound the wailing of the wind. Weary Hannah slept on, while the sisters saw a pale shadow that seemed to fall upon the little bed. An hour went by and nothing happened except Laurie leaving for the station.

Another hour passed and still no one came. The girls were haunted by anxious fears of delay in the storm, or accidents by the way, or, worst of all, a great grief at Washington.

It was past four when Jo heard a movement by the bed. Turning quickly, she saw Meg with her face hidden. A dreadful fear passed coldly over Jo as she thought, *Beth is dead, and Meg is afraid to tell me.*

"The fever's turned!" Meg exclaimed, lifting her face, which shone with tears. "Look, Jo, Beth is breathing normally!"

Jo leaned over to check, and then she was crying too. It was true! Beth finally looked peaceful, her chest rising and falling evenly.

"If Marmee would only come now!" said Jo as the winter night began to wane.

Never had the sun risen so beautifully, and never had the world seemed so lovely as it did to the heavy eyes of Meg and Jo as they looked out in the early morning.

"It looks like a fairy world," said Meg. She smiled to herself as she stood behind the curtain watching the dazzling sight.

"Hark!" cried Jo, jumping to her feet.

Yes, there was a sound of bells at the door below, a cry from Hannah, and then Laurie's voice saying in a joyful whisper, "Girls, she's come! She's come!"

14.

The peaceful weeks that followed were like sunshine after a storm. Beth was soon able to lie on the study sofa all day, playing with her cats and sewing new clothes for all her little dolls.

Beth's once active limbs were so stiff and feeble that Jo carried her for a daily airing about the house in her strong arms. Meg cooked cakes for "the dear," cheerfully burning her white hands as she did so, while Amy celebrated her own return by giving away as many of her treasures as she could get Beth to accept.

As Christmas approached, thoughts turned to this year's festivities, and Jo began to propose utterly impossible or ridiculous ceremonies in honor of this oddly merry Christmas.

Laurie was just as excited and would have had bonfires, skyrockets, and grand arches if he'd had his own way. There were many arguments, and the rest of the family finally thought they had changed the minds of the ambitious pair, who went about with forlorn faces for a day or two. But the explosions of laughter soon returned when the two got together again.

Several days of strangely mild weather ushered in a splendid Christmas Day. To begin with, Mr. March wrote that he should soon be with them, then Beth felt uncommonly well that morning. She was dressed in her mother's gift of a soft crimson dressing gown when Jo brought her to the window to see her and Laurie's offering.

Like elves, Jo and Laurie had worked through the night and created a comical surprise. Out in the garden stood Meg, dressed as a stately snow maiden, crowned with holly, holding a basket of fruit and flowers in one hand, and a great roll of sheet music in the other. An enormous rainbow of a blanket was wrapped around Meg, and she began to sing through chattering teeth.

"God bless you, dear Queen Beth, may nothing you dismay . . ." Meg sang. The carol turned into a list of gifts for Beth, which Jo, Amy, and Laurie kept darting in with. There were fruit, flowers, the big rainbow blanket, music for the piano, a portrait of Jo painted by Amy, a red ribbon for her kitten's tail, and a pail of ice cream that Meg had made herself.

How Beth laughed when she saw it all, how they all ran up and down to bring in the gifts, and what ridiculous speeches Jo made as she presented them.

"I'm so full of happiness that I couldn't hold one drop more, even if Father were here," said Beth, sighing with contentment. Jo carried her off to the study to rest after the excitement, and to refresh herself with some of the delicious grapes the snow maiden had sent her.

"So am I," added Jo.

"I'm sure I am," echoed Amy.

"Of course I am!" cried Meg, who had changed into her first silk dress, for Mr. Laurence had insisted on giving it as a Christmas gift.

"How can I be otherwise?" said Mrs. March gratefully as her eyes moved from her husband's letter to Beth's smiling face.

Now and then, in this ordinary world, things do happen that seem too good to be true, and what a comfort it is. It was half an hour after everyone had said they were so happy they couldn't hold one drop more, and the drop came.

Laurie opened the parlor door and popped his head in very quietly. He might just as well have turned a somersault, because his face was so full of excitement and his voice so joyful. Everyone jumped up, and he said, in a strange, breathless voice, "Here's another Christmas present for the March family."

Before the words were out of Laurie's mouth, he was whisked away somehow. In his place appeared a tall man, with a scarf up to the eyes, leaning on the arm of Mr. Brooke, who tried to say something and couldn't.

"Father!" Jo shrieked.

Of course there was a general stampede. For several minutes everybody seemed to lose their wits, for the strangest things were done and no one said a word.

Mr. March became invisible as four pairs of loving arms embraced him. Jo disgraced herself by nearly fainting away. Mr. Brooke kissed Meg but entirely by mistake, as he tried to explain. And Amy tumbled over a stool but didn't stop to get up, instead hugging and crying over her father's boots.

Marmee was the first to recover herself and held up her hand with a warning, "Hush! Remember Beth."

But it was too late. The study door flew open and the little red dressing gown appeared on the threshold, joy putting strength into the weak limbs. Beth ran straight into her father's arms.

A hearty laugh set everybody straight again, for Hannah was discovered behind the door, sobbing as she held the fat turkey. She had forgotten to put it down when she rushed up from the kitchen.

As the laughter faded, Marmee began to thank Mr. Brooke for looking after her husband. At this point Mr. Brooke suddenly remembered that Mr. March was still recovering. Then the two invalids were ordered to rest, which they did, by both Father and Beth sitting in one big chair and talking hard. Mr. Brooke and Laurie slipped away, leaving the March family to catch up on these miraculous events.

Mr. March told how he had longed to surprise them, and how, when the fine weather came just before Christmas, he had been allowed by his doctor to take advantage of it. He explained how devoted Mr. Brooke had been, and how he was altogether a most admirable and upright young man.

Mr. March paused a minute just there and glanced at Meg, who was violently poking the fire. He looked at his wife with an enquiring lift of the eyebrows. Mrs. March gently nodded and asked if he wouldn't like to have something to eat. Jo saw and understood the look, and she stomped away to get wine and beef tea, muttering to herself as she slammed the door, "I hate admirable young men with brown eyes!"

There never was such a Christmas dinner as the Marches had that day. The fat turkey was a sight to behold when Hannah sent him up, stuffed, browned, and decorated. So was the plum pudding, which melted in one's mouth—likewise the jellies, which Amy enjoyed like a fly in a honeypot.

Mr. Laurence and his grandson dined with them, and also Mr. Brooke, at whom Jo scowled, to Laurie's amusement. Two easy chairs stood side by side at the head of the table, in which sat Beth and her father, feasting modestly on chicken and a little fruit. They drank to their healths, told stories, sang songs, remembered old times, and enjoyed themselves greatly. A sleigh ride had been planned, but the girls would not leave their father, so the guests departed early. As twilight gathered, the happy family sat together around the fire.

"Just a year ago we were groaning over the horrible Christmas we expected to have. Do you remember?" asked Jo.

"It's been rather a pleasant year on the whole!" said Meg. She smiled at the fire and congratulated herself on having treated Mr. Brooke with dignity.

"I think it's been a pretty hard one," said Amy, watching the fire with thoughtful eyes.

"I'm glad it's over, because we've got you back," whispered Beth, who sat on her father's knee.

"And I'm glad to begin another year with my dear, dear girls," Mr. March said. "God bless my little women!"

Author's Note

Some readers will already be familiar with the story of *Little Women* thanks to the many film and television adaptations that exist of the book. The most recent film adaptation, released in 2019, was nominated for six Oscars, including Best Picture, and demonstrates the enduring appeal of this wonderful novel.

If you do know the story, then you may be surprised by the ending of this retelling.

The first volume of *Little Women* was published in 1868 and was an instant success. Three months after the first book was published, Louisa May Alcott wrote a second volume of the story (often published separately in the UK with the title *Good Wives*). Adaptations for the screen tend to combine both stories—including the next part of the March sisters' lives, picking up three years later. We see the sisters fall in love, find new beginnings, and face devastating loss.

This retelling has been created with a specific goal in mind: to make Alcott's original novel accessible to readers who may otherwise struggle to read it. The combined length of Alcott's original books made them far too long to fit into this format, and so this retelling focuses only on book one.

Our books are tested
for children and young people by
children and young people.

Thanks to everyone who consulted on
a manuscript for their time and effort in
helping us to make our books better
for our readers.

Get lost in timeless classic retellings.

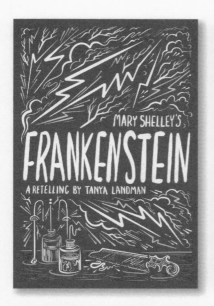

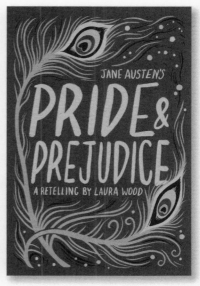

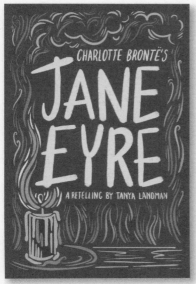

EVERYONE CAN BE A READER